Attack on Titan

The Harsh Mistress of the City

Part 2

Created by Hajime Isayama

A Novel by Ryo Kawakami

Art by Range Murata

Translated by Jonathan Lloyd-Davies

VERTICAL.

First published in Japan in 2015 by Kodansha, Ltd., Tokyo
Publication for this English edition arranged through Kodansha, Ltd., Tokyo
English language version produced by Vertical, Inc.

Art by Range Murata.

Originally published in Japanese as *Shingeki no Kyojin: Kakuzetsu Toshi no Jouou 2.*

This is a work of fiction.

ISBN: 978-1-942993-29-2

Manufactured in the United States of America

First Edition

Vertical, Inc.
451 Park Avenue South
7th Floor
New York, NY 10016
www.vertical-inc.com

The Harsh Mistress of the City

CONTENTS

CHAPTER FOUR — 7
CHAPTER FIVE — 111
EPILOGUE — 193

COMMENTARY — 203

The Harsh Mistress of the City

CHAPTER FOUR

A tepid wind blew over Rita's skin.

She was standing on the balcony outside the windows. A broad wooden platform had been assembled at the end, reaching out towards the circular plaza.

The platform was a gallows.

Below, a great crowd of civilians filled the plaza to capacity. They could be seen even in the windows of the buildings enclosing the space. The air was alive with a low, thrumming excitement. Only the space in front of the district hall remained empty, in a gaping semicircle.

In the center was a Titan.

Presently it sat like a baby, with its haunches on the ground and its legs thrust out. At a glance it approximated a chubby, middle-aged man, but it was over five meters tall. Its straight hair fell around its jawline in a sort of bob. Its flattish features were marked with a melancholic look.

Of course, a Titan's expressions signified nothing. The creatures had no capacity for thought or emotion.

All they had was their craving to feed on people.

The Titan's neck, waist, and limbs were weighed down with dense chains that snaked off into the surrounding area. There were dozens in total. Each fed into a powerful winding mechanism, contraptions as large as a bull originally used to open and close the wall gates. Numerous stakes secured them into the cobblestones.

With the chains exerting their force from every direction, the Titan was utterly incapable of movement. Only its melancholic eyes shifted now and then, rolling up, down, right, and left.

Even then nobody tried to approach it.

It was hardly surprising. What if a few of the chains were close to breaking? What if the winding mechanisms proved faulty? What if the Titan possessed far greater strength than they had supposed?

If it did somehow break free, a civilian would have no means of fighting back.

"Forgive me… I'm sorry! I won't do it again. Please, I promise!"

Rita turned slowly towards the voice behind her. A middle-aged man was squirming, restrained by soldiers. His greasy hair was flat on his forehead. Looking around forty and out of shape, his appearance wasn't unlike that of the Titan below. Only the look in his eyes was different. They blazed with an abnormal intensity mixing horror and desperation.

Among the soldiers was Amanda. White-skinned, with long

black hair and tapered eyes, she was younger than twenty but looked mature beyond her years. This was in stark contrast to Rita, who had childlike features with short and unruly locks of blond hair.

Amanda had been talented from the start, skilled in combat and quick-witted. But she had lacked a certain dedication and exhibited a poor attitude towards her superiors, so the Garrison had appointed Rita team leader before her. As a result, Rita was acting commander of the Garrison in Quinta District right then.

It had been half a year since she first assumed the role.

"I beg you. Please…" the man pleaded with tears in his voice.

The soldiers didn't answer. Silently they pressed him forwards.

The man came to a stop beside Rita.

The excitement was growing in the crowd, the commotion rising in volume.

"Please. You can't do this. I don't want to be eaten…"

"This man…" the soldier handling the sentencing read the man's name aloud. Holding up the document containing the charges, he took a step forwards to flank the condemned on the other side from Rita.

Naturally, the soldier was younger than her. Young enough to still be a boy. The majority of the soldiers were his age. If not for that, Rita, who wasn't even twenty herself, could never have become the Garrison's acting commander.

She found herself remembering a boy who'd died half a year ago.

He had been a soldier too. A valued assistant, who had held her in particular admiration.

But he was gone.

Having stumbled onto a group of thieves, he'd attempted to make an arrest, only to face resistance and have half his head unceremoniously blown away.

Rita could never let such a tragedy happen again.

That was why she needed to establish absolute order. She had to transform the way people thought. She needed to convince them all that it didn't pay to break the law, that a pure and just life of selfless devotion was the choice route to happiness.

"...has stolen enough food, including a hunk of pork and a tub of butter, to last a family of four through a week. Moreover..." the boy soldier continued to list the man's charges.

Considered in isolation they were perhaps trivial, yet in this man's case the charges were particularly numerous. No matter how many times they arrested him, he ended up committing similar crimes again.

At this stage, he was beyond reprieve.

The boy soldier paused when he had finished reading the charges. He took a deep breath, then declared the sentence.

"For these crimes we hereby proceed to execute him!"

His voice had turned shrill.

"Then just kill me. I won't ask for forgiveness, not anymore… but please kill me here, now! I beg you!"

The man began to struggle, but his hands were tied behind his back with rope, and two well-built soldiers had him firmly by the wrists and shoulders. He pitched his head left then right, but there was no one willing to meet his gaze.

"Come on…"

There were tears in his eyes, his nose was running, and saliva dribbled from his mouth.

Rita noticed a foul smell. The man had voided his bowels. The younger soldiers didn't even try to hide their grimaces.

Rita focused on breathing through her mouth.

Lifting the man, the soldiers forced him over the railing at the end of the balcony. They followed him over and continued forwards along the wooden slats of the platform.

"How tasteless," Amanda muttered.

"That could be construed as treason," Rita calmly countered, still facing forwards.

She crossed the railing and strode across the platform to stand next to the soldiers. It ended just ahead of their position.

Beyond this, slightly lower down, was the Titan's face. It was looking up, studying Rita and the others, its melancholic expression unchanged. Its lips and eyes almost seemed to be glittering in the powerful glare of the sun.

Its eyes squarely met Rita's.

Perhaps it hated her, perhaps it did not—she couldn't tell.

The Titan had shown up five months earlier, alone, in the vicinity of Quinta's exterior wall. Seemingly devoid of purpose, it had been trudging through the abandoned shantytown, most of which had been razed to the ground in a bombardment. Rita and Amanda had confronted the creature with the aim of killing it. It was only blind chance that had led them to capture it alive.

They had been unable to work in chorus during the battle because Rita had lost all sense of self-composure. It hadn't been long since the loss of her boy soldier aide, Duccio.

How could anyone have expected her to stay in control?

Shortly after the battle had begun, their respective anchors impaled the Titan's gut and back. Wires trailed from the anchors to the winding mechanisms the pair wore.

The Titan responded with ponderous but unpredictable movements, dragging Rita and Amanda. They slammed into the hard ground and tumbled through the debris. They sustained injuries all over their bodies.

But the result, they realized, was a Titan trapped in the wires wrapped around its body.

Rita and Amanda summoned their subordinates, and they reinforced the restraints on the creature and hauled it back into Quinta.

If the angle of the anchors had been off by even a fraction, and if the Titan hadn't been alone, the battle might have seen an altogether different end. Chances were that one of them, possibly both, would have lost their lives.

For the next month they kept the Titan confined within the Garrison premises, relatively close to the gate. They did perform experiments to learn more about Titan behavior, but since the district lacked experts, it didn't amount to much.

The decision to move the Titan to the plaza was Rita's.

This monster will become a symbol of order—the thought had come abruptly and without warning one day.

Rita was glad for it.

And here, right now, she would again prove the value of her idea.

She regarded the Titan below, then raised her right hand up above her head. The gaze of the crowd focused in on that single point, her hand. The low chattering had completely died away.

There was only the sound of the wind, and the gentle weeping of the man about to be executed.

He began to struggle again. He squirmed in the arms of the soldiers, frothed at the mouth, shouted incoherently. The soldiers were unperturbed. They were used to it.

Rita swung down her arm.

The soldiers at either side of the man took hold of his waist and shoulders. Hoisting him into the air, they swung him momentarily back towards the district hall before hurling him as far as they could into the plaza. At the same time, the troops next to the winding mechanisms rolled a couple of meters of slack into the Titan's chains. The metal made a screeching noise as it was unwound.

The Titan was quick to notice its leeway.

It trembled, and its back snapped straight.

The man fell from above, pitifully flailing his arms and legs.

Its own arms granted a temporary freedom, the Titan raised one as if to make a toast, and opened its mouth. The inside was lined with rows of yellowed teeth, each the size of a human fist. A slimy tongue writhed there, and beyond was darkness.

Rita felt as though she'd glimpsed the bottom of a deep well.

With unexpected speed, the Titan snatched at the man from two sides. Its right hand grabbed the man's head, its left his knees. In one deft movement the Titan flipped the man into a horizontal position and sank its jaw into his still-clothed buttocks.

There was a horrific cry and a gush of blood. The stones below were stained red. The spray of blood also struck the underside of the platform where Rita and the others stood, pattering like rain on a rooftop.

The next sound they heard was the crunching of bone.

The man's desperate screams had trailed off. He must have fainted immediately.

Already finished with his rump, the Titan was on to the side of his belly. Blood and viscera spattered out. A repulsive rhythm, of the monster masticating, reached their ears.

All signs of life were gone from the man's eyes. His body freely came apart at the middle.

The Titan lifted the upper half high into the air and supped, melancholically, at the blood and viscera dripping down. Then it tossed the portion whole into its mouth after all.

The lower half met more or less the same fate.

The plaza had fallen completely silent. But it wasn't over yet.

He was only the first.

"Next!" the cracked voice of a soldier came from behind Rita.

She turned to face it. The soldiers at her side went back into the building. Another two appeared in their place, holding the next man and conveying him forwards.

Unlike the one before him he put up no resistance, nor begged for his life to be spared. He was perfectly at ease; if anything, his eyes seemed to betray concern for Rita. This one also had long hair, but he didn't come across as louche. There was something of the artist about him. He looked to be in his mid-forties, and his clothes and shoes were old, but in good condition.

Henning Iglehaut.

Rita's adoptive father. Until recently, she had believed him to be her true father.

The soldiers dragged him until he stood at the edge of the platform. Across from them, the boy soldier raised another sheet into the air. He read out Henning's name, then began to list the charges.

"...who, in the three months leading to his arrest, facilitated the suicides of at least sixteen men and women by supplying lethal drugs..."

Rita took out a thumb-sized vial and glanced down at it. There was liquid inside, still up to the cork. A depression, wound with a long leather cord, allowed it to be worn around the neck. Henning had been selling them—vials of poison—to all who wished to take their own lives.

As an experienced apothecary, Henning had sometimes prepared drugs to put down wild dogs and other dangerous animals. Making poison capable of killing a man wouldn't have been any more complicated.

"Why?" Rita couldn't help but mutter.

She saw suicide as an act of denying one's current circumstances. In other words, it was a denial of the "ordered world" she was working to build. She couldn't tolerate anyone who promoted such behavior.

Why had Henning thought to resume his manufacture of the poison? Why did everyone have to betray her?

The moment and scene of Duccio's shooting death resurrected itself in her mind. Blood and brain matter spilling from his skull, and, beyond, the face of her dear—her once dear—childhood friend...

The boy soldier, his voice turning shrill again, declared, "For these crimes, we hereby proceed to execute him!"

Henning turned his head and said across the soldiers, “I don’t regret what I’ve done.”

Rita gave no answer.

Undeterred, Henning added, “I believe it’s important to give people a way out, if they need it.”

Wrong. It was wrong for anyone to seek a way out. The people of Quinta needed to all come together and work towards the realization of a better world.

Rita lifted her right hand in silence.

“You’re really going through with this?” Amanda asked from behind. She had crossed the railing at some point to join them on the platform.

Rita remained silent.

Henning spoke again, his tone chiding: “You need to forgive him.” He was referring to her childhood friend, Mathias Kramer, who had shot and killed Duccio. “There has to be an explanation. It must have been an accident.”

“Immaterial.”

The soldiers were pretending not to hear, looking away from both Henning and Rita. No doubt, they did know that the two were related. That they were parent and child. Even if they weren’t related by blood, they were profoundly close.

Yet, Rita couldn’t let him go. The soldiers, who were still very young, mustn’t be allowed to think that she’d extended mercy to family.

She let her eyes drop beyond the edge of the platform. The Titan was gazing up with the same despondent look. The area around its mouth was dirty with blood and flesh. There were strands of hair on its lips. The cobblestones beneath were wet with large quantities of milky saliva and scattered with bloody chunks of meat.

The end for those who broke the law.

Titans did not devour people out of hunger. Once they were finished chewing, instead of swallowing they spat out the meat. Nobody knew why.

The Titan stirred. It made to lift its head in Rita's direction. But the winding mechanisms had pulled the chains tight again, leaving the creature hardly able to budge. The taut links trembled a fraction, creaking ominously.

Rita looked back at Henning.

"Goodbye."

With that, she brought her hand down.

For a moment Henning looked apprehensive. Not because he feared death itself, she knew. Rather, he feared dying and leaving Rita behind.

Then you shouldn't have betrayed me in the first place.

The soldiers lifted Henning into the air, but somewhat hesitantly. They were ready for Rita to declare a stay of execution.

But she only watched, silent.

Making up their minds, the young soldiers awkwardly tossed

Henning into the air. On cue, chains went slack all across the plaza.

With an agility that belied its preceding state, the Titan jutted out its chin and chomped down on Henning's thighs. Wrenching him downwards with a nod, it gripped his slender frame in its freed hands. Angling its neck, it feasted on the soft belly of a human. The creature was proceeding with its meal much like before.

Henning kept his eyes on Rita until the end. His belly torn open, devoured, that was where his body snapped in two.

Rita watched it all without looking away.

***

"What the...?"

Gabriele crouched in the shadow of the undergrowth and squinted into the dark, cocking his head to one side. Several men and women were moving around under the moonlight. There were no torches or other forms of light. They seemed to be picking fruit from the trees, grabbing carelessly; none of them looked like farmers.

Gabriele could just about make out their whispered voices.

"Hurry it up. Be done in two hours."

"I'm kind of tired..."

"Just shape up, okay?"

The atmosphere didn't seem particularly cordial.

Wall Maria had fallen to a Titan attack half a year earlier. As a result, mankind had been forced to abandon all territory outside of Wall Rose. While the majority of residents had evacuated towards the interior, others had, needless to say, been left stranded. Perhaps the people ahead of him belonged to that group of survivors "wandering between the walls."

Even then, the district at Wall Maria's westernmost point, Quinta—abandoned at one point, but with a great many people still living inside, Gabriele had heard—was within arm's reach.

Why hadn't they gone to ask for help? What were they doing wasting time in a place like this?

What did they hope to do if they were set upon by an "aberrant" Titan?

Had they been denied entry?

Such a thing was possible. Quinta would have limited supplies of food. Naturally, they might lack the capacity to take people in from outside.

No, wait… If that was true, why were they gathering food here, so close to the district? Was it some display against Quinta?

Titans were drawn to areas with a high population density. This was a well-known fact. If these people couldn't get through the wall, their best chance of survival was to get as far away from the town as possible.

So—why were they still here?

Doesn't make any sense.

The daytime heat was enough to keep one sweating, but it cooled by night. The rustling of the leaves was soothing to hear.

Gabriele continued watching. With no clouds in the sky, the moonlight provided all the brightness he needed. No one in view looked to be armed. They carried baskets and wooden boxes for the fruit they were picking, but Gabriele couldn't make out any other possessions. None looked like they'd spent the last half-year since the fall of Wall Maria in the exterior.

Gabriele adjusted the sack slung over his back. It contained a change of clothes, some food, water, and arms. He got the feeling the group was larger than the few people he could see picking fruit up ahead. He could sense more, beyond the layers of trees. Ten, twenty, maybe more still, all busy and working.

It was a substantial gathering.

Well, watching won't get me anywhere.

His decision made, Gabriele got to his feet and stepped into the moonlight. Making sure his footsteps were audible, he approached the group of men and women. They hadn't looked to be armed, but he had no guarantee they wouldn't attack if they mistook him for a wild dog or an aberrant Titan.

It always paid to be careful.

A male and female pair, both of them short, noticed his approach first. They both stopped what they were doing and turned to face him head-on, seemingly raising their guard a fraction.

They were young. Gabriele had only just turned twenty himself, but they were probably around the same age.

"Who are you?" the male asked. He had sharp eyes and wore a terribly annoyed expression. There was something mocking in his attitude.

Gabriele was lanky with features that were more juvenile than not, and it often led people to mistake him for a younger man. This fellow, too, had probably decided he was a pushover.

Gabriele didn't like it, but this wasn't the time to pick a fight. He suppressed his irritation and accosted the pair.

"My name is Gabriele. What are you two—"

"Don't know it. Which team?"

"Team?"

"You get separated? Or—"

"Are you thinking of making a run for it?" the woman cut in, her voice oddly cheerful.

She was short but shapely. Her face was framed in soft, lightly colored hair. She wore a barely perceptible grin that looked like it might be a permanent feature, but also had an aloof manner that was difficult to pin down.

Gabriele asked in response, "Run? Where to?" Where could you run in a world prowling with Titans?

The woman cocked her head sideways, her eyes coming to stop on his sack. "Uh…and what's that? Where'd you get that?"

"I didn't *get it* anywhere… We're not communicating so well, are we?"

"You're not one of the residents?" The man's eyes were gradually widening. "You came here from outside?"

"Yeah. How should I… Well." He wanted to hear their story first but supposed it a good idea to set them at ease. He gathered his thoughts and spoke slowly. "I've been out here by myself, on the run since Titans attacked my village. Every day I've been grabbing food from empty houses, pulling vegetables from fields. Just like you guys…" He pointed at what he guessed was an orchard. "Picking fruit and all that. 'Course, the moment I even glimpse a Titan I run as fast as I can, and I make sure I only move around at nighttime."

The Titans were diurnal. Discounting some "aberrant" types, there was almost no chance of coming across one at night.

"Make sense?"

"Sure."

"So, you're all from Quinta?"

The man had been surprised to discover that Gabriele wasn't from the district. This suggested the group was from the town. By now, the others had stopped what they were doing and begun to pay close attention to the exchange between Gabriele and the two who had seen him first.

The man with the sharp eyes said, "Yes."

The short woman gave Gabriele an approving look. "It's amazing you survived half a year. Out here, without even a horse."

"Oh, I had a horse! Found a stray, guess its master had died. That was lucky. Steeds cost like you wouldn't believe, right? But it got away this morning. I thought I was in real trouble, and then I noticed your group."

"Even so, it's impressive."

This was one of the other men. He put his box on the ground and proceeded to plod over. Chubby in typical middle-aged fashion, he had long greasy hair that was tied back in a ponytail.

"I'll bet you've got a good idea about the state of things outside the wall."

"The state of things *between* the walls, if we're being picky. But yeah, I've got a pretty good idea."

"I'm sure our guy would want to hear what the man's got to say," the middle-aged man with the long hair said, turning to face the other two.

"Yeah. Always bursting with curiosity, isn't he," the woman agreed, her tone ever casual.

The sharp-eyed man's continued distrust was in stark contrast to this. "Who cares what he wants, but it might serve some use. Either way it's better than letting that woman get hold of him."

The man with the long hair nodded. "So let's bring him in. Shouldn't be hard, if we've got a runaway tonight."

"Sorry, who's 'our guy'? And while we're at it, 'that woman'?" Gabriele asked, but no one made to speak.

They were all looking at him with appraising eyes. It wasn't pleasant, to say the least. He tried another question.

"Why are you all outside the wall, anyway? Are things that bad inside? Have you run out of food?"

"I guess you could say it's bad, yeah," the man with the long hair answered vaguely.

"Yup," the short woman shrugged, "it's a bit complicated."

"Sure doesn't look straightforward with you out here…"

"Follow me, I'll fill you in," the sharp-eyed man said, turning on his heels without waiting for Gabriele to respond, taking his acquiescence for granted.

Gabriele overheard the short woman mumble, "Guess we're not canvassing this time."

He had no idea what she meant.

The sharp-eyed man introduced himself as Klaus. Taking the lead, he wove a path through the trees. He seemed to be aiming for another group.

The short woman had volunteered to join them and puffed up her cheeks when Klaus told her he'd be fine by himself. In the end she'd been convinced to stay and carry on picking fruit with the others.

Klaus walked along briskly. The dark seemed to give him no anxiety whatsoever.

After a while they drew closer to multiple voices and figures.

Here, too, they were engaged in harvesting, but in comparison to Klaus' group their movements were sluggish. They exuded a sense of fear and panic. Constantly monitoring their surroundings, they seemed to be jumping at every little noise.

In fact, it was their behavior that was normal.

"Any runaways?" Klaus called out to a man nearby.

He left a tree where most of the fruit had been picked and shook his head. "No, not tonight. Everyone here's married. I doubt anyone's thinking of escaping by themselves."

"I see, thanks."

Klaus began to walk, keeping up the same brisk pace. Not once did he turn to look at Gabriele.

No runaways. Everyone here's married. Did that mean they all had dependents back in Quinta? *Nah, that's not enough, I need more information.*

"Hey. Didn't you say you were going to fill me in on what's happening?"

"Just as you see," replied Klaus, threading doggedly between the trees, "we're picking fruit. Some days we gather vegetables, others we go after beasts. Regardless of what we're doing, it's called the Night Harvest."

"I can see that… But is it really that bad? The food supply, in Quinta," Gabriele asked, ducking under some low-hanging fruit. "I mean it's relatively safe at night, sure, but we know there are aberrants, and there's always the chance you might stumble into a regular Titan. Do you really need to do this?" Another group came into view, also engaged in the so-called Night Harvest. "Putting so many people's lives in danger? What if you were all wiped out? Food can't compensate for that. What are the higher-ups thinking?"

Klaus suddenly stopped and turned to stare at him.

"What?" Gabriele came to a halt as well.

"So you really don't know?"

"That's what I've been trying to tell you."

They locked eyes under the moonlight.

Klaus snorted, then looked into the distance. "Okay, fair enough."

"Enough drama. Just tell me."

"You must know Wall Maria was breached?"

"Of course I do."

Hordes of Titans had crossed into the territory between Wall Rose and Wall Maria. Gabriele had eluded many in person, somehow managing to arrive here.

Klaus nodded, then continued, "Half of Quinta's population was evacuated to Wall Rose, but the other half didn't make it in time. They ended up trapped inside."

"That part I understand. But you lost half your population. That means you only need half the food supplies. Why on earth would you have to—"

"The food situation is grave. But you're right, not so grave that we have to do this."

Klaus started walking again.

The Night Harvest continued around them. The men and women appeared tired but in a way that seemed more mental than physical. They were all dressed differently, but none were particularly ragged. The impression they gave was that of being ordinary townsfolk.

Glancing at the Night Harvest, Klaus muttered, "This is nothing but a tool, for that woman to maintain power."

"Really? You mentioned her before. Who the hell is 'that woman'?"

"A Garrison soldier currently in charge of Quinta. Her name is Rita Iglehaut. She's young, only in the position she is because all the senior officers died or made a run for it."

"Why have you got a soldier in charge? Normally it'd be a government official."

"They were the first to leave."

Gabriele clucked his tongue. He couldn't believe their cowardice. "Okay…"

"The Night Harvest is mandatory for all civilians. Shifts come in fixed intervals and include every able-bodied adult. The exception is anyone who disrupts the peace. They get a higher proportion of shifts."

"Hence this being a tool to maintain power. To make an example of people, I see…" It made sense. "I'd been wondering why you would do something this dangerous. But it's a calculated move. She's forcing people to engage in a frightening task—so she can rule by terror."

"'Rule by terror'..." Klaus contemplated Gabriele's phrase. "You're right. And she's got a particular gift for it."

"But why go this far? Quinta's in crisis, surely the people would listen without her having to resort to this kind of thing. Is it that unruly inside?"

"Not at all. If anything, it's so orderly it's freakish. She's obsessed with keeping it that way."

"Sounds like a good thing to me?"

"It's a question of degree. The way it is now, not even the slightest misdemeanor is permitted. The punishment for stealing, of course, is severe, but also for cutting in line at rations, for spitting on the ground, for badmouthing the troops. And people are being encouraged to inform on others."

"That sucks."

"Yeah. It sucks."

"I suppose that is out of whack. People must feel pretty frustrated. She uses the fear of harsh punishment to keep them in line, then."

"I should clarify," Klaus said, surveying the orchard and the frightened people working there, "that this is our duty. We aren't being punished."

"The actual punishments are much worse. Is that what you

want to say?"

"You'll see soon enough."

"Not sure I want to."

"Right, then." Again, Klaus stopped amongst some trees. They were positioned a fair distance from each group of harvesters. Klaus had no doubt chosen the spot so they wouldn't be overheard. "What do you think?"

"About?"

"The current state of the town."

"Sounds crap."

"You really think so?"

"Of course, however you look at it, it's crap. Why even ask?"

"Just checking." Dropping his eyes to his feet, Klaus ran his hand over the surface of one of the trees. "What was your name?"

"Gabriele."

"Right. Gabriele, you've got two paths to choose from. You could continue to the gate, explain everything to the soldiers, and ask for shelter. Do that, and that woman would be interested in hearing everything you have to say."

"I don't know anything important."

"You probably know things you don't even realize. You know about the state of things out here. That's valuable info."

"What's the second path?"

"We get a lot of runaways. People who've had enough of all the crap, to use your term. There'll no doubt be one or two tonight. You assume one of their identities and enter Quinta instead of them. From then on you live without a name."

"Any advantages at all to the second path?"

Klaus used his eyes to motion around them. "You wouldn't be sent out to do this," he said of the Night Harvest.

"Okay, I guess that's actually quite big."

"And you wouldn't need to worry for food or a place to sleep. We'll work something out for you."

"Why would you go that far to help me?"

"We want to know what's up outside of town, too."

"I just told you, I don't know anything of use."

"And so? Which path do you choose?" pressed Klaus.

Gabriele brought to mind their earlier exchanges. Klaus' team had a noticeably different attitude and mood compared to the others. Come to think of it, the short and carefree woman had spoken about "canvassing" people.

"I see. I think I get it now."

Klaus, for his part, wasn't making any particular effort to hide what he was doing. Maybe he was testing Gabriele's wits, his powers of observation.

If so, I should prove that I'm no fool.

"You disapprove of the status quo," he said. "You want to mix things up a little. By force. You're amassing comrades to that end."

"Who knows?" Klaus declined to confirm.

A cautious fellow. Gabriele adjusted the position of his sack. "Sure, sounds fun. Count me in."

"Meaning?"

"I choose the second path. I'll help you out."

"I don't recall asking for help."

A cautious fellow, thought Gabriele, *but also a pain in the ass.*

Dawn was beginning to show on the horizon.

The fear seemed to thicken as it rose from the crowd. One could almost smell it. They were all returning towards the gate, each carrying heaps of fruit, each jockeying to be the first in line. Gabriele was lending a hand, helping carry Klaus' basket, which was packed to the brim with fruit. He'd left the sack he'd had with him back in the orchard. It wasn't as though it had contained anything of value.

Eventually the black mass of the wall came into view. Fifty meters high. Perhaps it would have been visible through the trees at night, but it had blended too well into the darkness for Gabriele to notice.

Chains held up the gate's iron-plated door. The entrance was three meters high, another three wide. It gave way to a cave-like passageway that had a curved ceiling. Two soldiers were stationed at each flank, checking names to papers in their hands, letting the people through one by one. The gatekeepers looked considerably young. They were in their mid-teens, possibly even in their early teens.

Those who had already arrived formed a line that all but clung to the wall in the half-dark. No doubt they were trying to get as close to "the inside world" and as far from "the outside world" where the Titans roamed as they could. The behavior was pointless, but Gabriele didn't fail to understand the sentiment behind it.

He joined the line with Klaus.

The wall next to them, built from old stone, was heavily marked. Gabriele knew that a huge number of Titans had swarmed in around it half a year ago. The scarring could have resulted from the Titans' nails or from stray shells during a bombardment. Then again, it was possibly natural delapidation over the course of time.

A middle-aged couple stood ahead of them, while a couple of youths, probably brothers, waited behind. The others from Klaus' team were farther back. The short and slippery woman went, it seemed, by the name of Nikki. She and Klaus appeared to be in charge of the rest of their company.

At Klaus' bidding, Gabriele put down their basket, then wiped the sweat from his forehead with his sleeve.

"You sure they won't notice?"

"Calm down."

"I am calm, but still."

They hadn't had any runaways that night, so Gabriele would

take the name of someone who had passed through the gate before him. Since the name was common, the chances of being suspected were low, he'd been assured.

"The runaways you've had so far..." Gabriele started.

"Too loud."

"Sorry." Gabriele moved closer to Klaus and lowered his voice. "But really, the runaways. What happens to them?"

"I'd like to ask you the same. I've been in here the whole time, half a year." Klaus indicated the wall with his eyes.

"Right. Fair enough."

"You didn't see any? Outside." Klaus was asking if anyone who might be a runaway had crossed paths with Gabriele as he'd drifted in the exterior.

He shrugged. "Now and then I caught sight of people like me. Just running from one place to the next, like they had nowhere to go, it looked like. Can't really say if they were runaways or not."

"Right." Klaus bent down and took hold of the basket. The line was moving again. He murmured, "I suppose most of them are dead. Eaten by Titans."

"Probably."

"You're a rare example. It's not normal for someone to last half a year."

"I was just lucky."

"Yeah. I can see that."

Gabriele was already growing accustomed to Klaus' sarcasm and antagonism. They moved forwards carried by the flow of people. Their turn came faster than expected.

Klaus went ahead and spoke to the soldiers first. He gruffly gave an unfamiliar name. Gabriele was confused for a moment but realized soon enough—Klaus, himself, had been out on a false identity. He'd given Gabriele his real name so readily, assuming "Klaus" was his real name, because he'd decided it was safe to do so.

"Proceed."

The soldier jerked his chin towards the passageway. Klaus carried the basket for three steps, then came to a stop.

Gabriele was next to stand between the soldiers. He gave them the name Klaus had prepped him with. He was surprised at how easily it rolled off his tongue.

He'd always been a good liar.

One of the soldiers glanced at his papers then ran a finger down the list of names. He looked back up and fixed Gabriele with a weary gaze.

Gabriele felt a rush of dread. He wondered if the soldier was about to ask who he really was. But the soldier remained silent, only tutting, and dropped his eyes back to his papers.

"Hurry up then," he said, terse, pointing beyond the gate with his chin.

Someone with the same name would have already gone

through, but the soldier had apparently decided this was a mistake in the ledger. With their focus on detecting runaways, they had failed to consider the possibility of someone like Gabriele trying to gain access from outside. It was hardly surprising; Quinta hadn't received a single visitor in the last half-year.

Feeling oddly let down, Gabriele exchanged a look with Klaus, then began to walk forwards.

The wall being close to ten meters thick at the base, it took a while to clear it. The ground was covered in stone and, with watch fires burning at regular intervals, it was considerably easier going than the outside.

Past the corridor, a broad thoroughfare led away in a straight line. Enormous brick buildings hugged the side of the wall. They looked like warehouses. Small crowds of people were gathered outside the entrances of each one.

"They used to belong to merchant associations, but the Garrison controls them now," Klaus, having picked up on Gabriele's interest, told him.

Taking directions from more soldiers, they carried the fruit they'd gathered into one of the warehouses. This doorway, too, was flanked with watch fires. The other buildings, probably residential, remained submerged in the penumbra. It seemed Quinta was yet to wake.

Some people broke away from the crowd and ran up to and embraced this or that basket bearer. They had to be family of the residents who had been out on the Night Harvest. Urged by the soldiers, the latter came away from their loved ones for the time being, carrying the fruit they'd gathered into the warehouse.

Gabriele and Klaus followed from behind. They climbed a low staircase and entered the building.

The ceiling was impressively high. The place was, it seemed, being used solely for storing fruit and vegetables. Gabriele's nose prickled at the smell of the raw produce. The wooden boxes and baskets were stowed directly on the floor. There were tall shelves to either side, but these were mainly empty. They didn't look like they'd be filled soon.

It was at least true, then, that the food situation was bad.

More soldiers had been posted by the walls inside, watchful so nobody attempted to make off with any of the food. They carried rifles with wooden stocks.

Ignoring them, Gabriele left the building with Klaus. He took a deep breath of Quinta. The air in the orchard was probably fresher, but somehow it felt more invigorating here. Perhaps it was the sense of security, the knowledge that he was protected by the wall.

"This way."

Klaus started off down the mostly empty thoroughfare.

"We're not waiting?"

Gabriele couldn't see Nikki and the others. He'd been sure the rest were coming along behind them, but it looked as though he'd been wrong.

Klaus didn't even look back. "We can't look conspicuous. We're going back separately."

"Where are we going?"

There was a pause.

"Our hangout," Klaus chose his words and answered.

It had to be their safe house, or something like it.

The temperature rose as they walked, and with it, the frequency with which they saw people out and about: a woman, probably a housewife, depositing trash in the street; an aging man probably on his way to work; and so on. Inside an eatery, a man who seemed to be its owner set about preparing for the day ahead. Gabriele saw merchants, too, carrying stock to such establishments. The food situation was doubtless bad, but Quinta's people didn't seem to be entirely dependent on rations.

Klaus turned a corner but stopped soon afterwards.

"Let's take a detour."

They returned to the avenue. After a while the view to the left opened up. There was a round, open space, some kind of plaza. It was vast. At the far side was a particularly grand building made of stone. A large wooden scaffolding covered its facade, perhaps for repairs on its outer wall.

And yet, there, in front of the scaffolding…

"What the hell is—"

"The district hall. That woman controls it now."

"No, I mean!"

"Need me to spell it out?"

No, I suppose not.

There was no mistaking it. It couldn't be anything else.

"Titan..."

There, in the center of the plaza, kneeled an unwashed, naked, and chubby man. Standing upright he would measure over five meters tall. Heavy chains spreading outwards in a radial pattern were wrapped around his neck, chest, belly, arms, wrists, and legs. Pulled tight and reflecting the pale morning light, the chains disappeared into machines that resembled tiny water mills. The apparatuses were bolted securely into the ground. There were twenty, maybe thirty of them in total.

A few heads short of ten soldiers, each carrying a rifle, stood around the perimeter.

"What is it doing here?" Gabriele's voice came out in a croak.

"Apparently that woman captured it."

Klaus was as blunt as ever. He didn't appear the slightest bit startled. Perhaps it was only normal, but he seemed fully accustomed to the outlandish spectacle.

"When you say 'that woman,' you mean that woman? The Garrison soldier."

"Yes."

"When did she...catch it?"

"Not long after Quinta's isolation. Less than a month."

"You hear stories now and then that such-and-such a place caught a Titan. Still, it's the first time I've seen one for real."

"Threw me too, first time I saw it."

"But keeping it here…it's dangerous. What if a child ventured too close by mistake? Say, is it on purpose? For people to vent their frustration, stoning it and that kind of thing?"

"Actually, it's the other way around."

"Other way? To keep them frustrated?"

"You're getting warmer. It's the same rationale as the Night Harvest."

"The same…"

"Doesn't seeing it scare you?"

The Titan hadn't budged the whole time. A few dozen chains held it tight. It could twitch but that was all. Only its eyes moved occasionally, while steam rose from its nose and mouth. The Titans had a body temperature that was incomparably higher than a human's.

"Of course it does. I'd be surprised to find anyone who felt fine."

"Agreed."

Klaus didn't seem particularly afraid. But he wasn't the type to lie or joke around. Maybe he was just bad at letting his emotions show.

"By putting that here—where everyone can see it—she's making sure the people of Quinta never forget their dread of the Titans. At the same time, she's reminding them that only the soldiers are capable of killing it."

"I see."

It was true—no civilians would be able to kill the Titan. Only the troops, with their training, were capable of that. They had special-purpose blades and knew how to gorge out its weak spot.

Gabriele swallowed. "So it's to issue a threat? 'Go against us and we'll set the Titan free…open the gate… We're the only ones who can protect you when that happens.'"

"Essentially. It's crude, but effective." Klaus turned around.

Gabriele stood there for a moment, entranced by the Titan, then hurried off after Klaus.

He decided it was true, that Rita Iglehaut—this woman who was in charge of Quinta—had a gift for intimidation. Who else would think to utilize something so horrific, so shocking and nightmarish, as a "proximate deterrent"?

They left the avenue to join a street lined on either side with private residences and two-story businesses. Many of these were brick. They continued for a while until they came upon a stone building, its entrance noticeably larger than the others, to the left. The doors had been left open. The majority of the pedestrians were drawn in through them.

Led by Klaus, Gabriele followed after them.

A roomy corridor ran straight down the center of the space,

with a patchwork of vendors set up at either side. Various goods were on display, including edibles, tobacco, liquor, garments, tableware, even furniture. Most of the stalls were still in the process of getting ready, but the ones that served food were already in business. Throngs of people stood examining the various commodities. In front of a cafe of sorts were simple chairs on which sat men holding cups of tea.

"A bazaar, huh?"

Gabriele had heard there were many covered markets in Quinta, but this had to be a particularly large one.

Klaus worked his way deeper inside, skillfully navigating a path through the flow of people and the characteristic aromas of tobaccos and spices.

"Don't get separated."

"Uh huh…"

Gabriele nearly collided with a man pushing a cart packed with garments and hurried out of the way.

"I thought Quinta was isolated. Where's all this stuff coming from?"

"Some of it is made in Quinta, some is what people had in stock. Some of it might be stolen goods. Half of Quinta's population left, after all."

"Makes sense. You can just rob an empty house…"

"You can. If you're happy to die, that is," jeered Klaus.

He entered an inconspicuous shop, almost buried among the

other businesses, located on the right at the end of a cul de sac. Old books lay in countless piles to either side of the doorway. It seemed to be a bookstore.

The inside was long and narrow, and down the center and against both walls were tall shelves, all of them crammed with books. The air carried their telltale dry smell. Gabriele took one at random and started to browse the pages.

"I trust you'll be careful with that, son."

Gabriele jumped at the closeness of the voice. Next to the entrance was a book-laden desk, behind which sat an aging man in glasses.

"Do take care not to drop or tear it."

"R-Right."

Was he the owner? As far as bookstores were concerned, trade didn't necessarily dwindle on account of Quinta's isolation.

"At the end."

Klaus strode past the shelves with unwavering steps. Gabriele peered down and saw an open corner at the back. Great numbers of books were piled directly on the floor. The impression they gave wasn't unlike a series of leaning towers. Although they looked ready to collapse, they somehow held stable. Among them, several men and women sat in a circle on stools. A few of them he'd met outside Quinta. They'd arrived before Gabriele and Klaus, presumably while they'd been examining the odious monster in the plaza.

"Is this him?" a young man seated near the wall spoke up.

He had closely cropped hair and a stubbly beard of around the same length. His forehead, on the broad side, lent him a somehow troubled expression. He was probably Gabriele's age. His right hand, splinted, was suspended by a piece of cloth—treatment for a broken bone. While he bore the outward resemblance of a working man, the way he carried himself hinted at refinement. Perhaps he came from a background of money or power—possibly both. Gabriele couldn't guess what might have brought about his fall.

Klaus tutted. "Stupid question. Who else would I bring here?"

"Of course. My mistake," the young man apologized, but didn't seem at all piqued. He seemed inured to Klaus' personality and attitude.

The young man looked Gabriele in the eye.

"It's good to meet you. My name is Mathias Kramer. I happen to represent this group."

His tone was gentle.

***

The day of his mother's funeral.

Mathias was sitting on his bed in his quarters and staring at empty space. Through the wall he could hear voices, the clinking of tableware. The guests who had arrived to offer their condolences were picking at snacks in the downstairs courtyard, making the rounds and reaffirming that they were "friends." He could count on his hand the number who were there to genuinely mourn. He wasn't even sure if it included his father, the deceased's husband, Jörg Kramer. For two days the senior Kramer had been so overwhelmed with preparations for the funeral, and now with keeping the mourners company, that he hadn't even had the time to make eye contact with his son.

Mathias was fourteen. At that age he was no longer a child, but neither was he an adult. While he had tried to be prepared, his mother's succumbing to illness had been a powerful blow. It was as though half his soul had been carved out and crushed. He had no confidence to keep going, to stand on his own two feet from tomorrow onwards.

He lacked the will to do anything at all.

Something hard hit the window. The one that faced the street outside. Mathias wondered if he was imagining things. Then he heard it again.

He turned his head slowly towards the sound. It felt like someone else was controlling his body.

A third crack.

Something was hitting the wooden shutters.

Mathias got woozily to his feet. He still didn't feel like he was moving of his own accord. Before he realized it he had crossed the room and opened the window, was poking his head out and peering down at the street.

Rita was looking up with concern on her face. She waved silently at Mathias. Then she started pointing at the ground. She wanted him to come down.

Mathias shook his head.

She repeated the gesture. Over and over, regardless of his protests.

Mathias pulled himself back into his quarters. He wanted to bury himself under his covers, but even that felt like too much of a struggle. Besides, Rita would only throw more stones at his window. It would be easier, he somehow decided then, to go out than to keep declining his friend's call. He went downstairs and headed towards the front door.

The guests showed no signs of noticing him.

He took the door to the street and found Rita waiting for him right outside.

"Let's take a walk," she suggested, a bit anxiously.

Mathias shook his head one more time.

Looking more decisive, Rita stepped forwards, reached out her arm, and seized him by the wrist. She started to walk, pulling him with her.

It was embarrassing to have a girl his own age tug him along like this. It felt like everyone around them was staring.

Before he knew it they were close to a bazaar. The eaves of the

various businesses formed a ceiling above them.

"Where are you…" *taking me?* he started to ask, but the answer came to him before he'd finished. Rita didn't have anywhere specific that she wanted to go. Her only purpose had been to get him out, to walk along with him like this.

They took a number of corners before coming out to a tiny open space with various shops around it. They passed before an ironmongers, then a soap makers. All the products on display were coated with a thick layer of dust.

"I lost my parents too," her confession came abruptly.

Mathias was puzzled. The gentle apothecary Henning. The spirited Doris. As far as he knew, her parents were alive and well.

He stopped. "What do you mean? Has something happened?" His hand came away from hers.

Rita stopped too, then turned around. "My current mother and father…aren't related to me by blood."

The area was quiet. There were no passersby or shop owners in sight.

"Why not?"

"My real mother, who gave birth to me…was in the Survey Corps. She died during one of her expeditions. My real father had trouble coping, so my current…sorry, I know this is confusing. He took some poison that Henning made. He killed himself."

"Sorry, wait… Henning? Poison?"

"Yes."

Rita looked away, focusing instead on the storefront of a bookshop that Mathias had visited a number of times. There was an old chair with a gray cat curled up on it.

"There were a lot of people in town who found life hard, who didn't want to keep going. I think there still are. My father used to put together a remedy that helped them die without pain. Without ever telling the royal government."

"But that's..."

If such a thing came to light, he was guaranteed the death penalty. Mathias doubted it was for the money. Henning must have believed that he was helping his clients.

Mathias didn't know what to say in response.

He could have brushed aside any straightforward attempts to comfort him. But this was something else.

"Don't worry," Rita spoke again. "He doesn't make it anymore."

"How long have you known this?"

"I only found out recently. Dad told me himself...and also that he'd given it without knowing my real father had a daughter."

"You mean the poison?"

"The poison. He only found out about me after my father was dead, and deeply regretted what he'd done. He stopped making the poison and started raising me, as my new father."

"Do you remember any of this?"

Rita shook her head. "Not really. It was so long ago. I think my memories of my real parents are all mixed up with my memories of Henning and Doris."

"But why tell you now? I mean, Henning could have kept it from you, if you didn't remember."

"I feel the same. And I think Mom…Doris, was against the idea. But he told me anyway, in secret."

"So Doris doesn't know—that you know."

"Probably not."

The cat yawned under Rita's gaze.

"Dad told me he didn't expect me to forgive him. My reserve corps exams were coming up. He said if I got through, I'd be able to leave home and never return if I didn't want to."

"But!"

Mathias' voice came out louder than expected. The cat pricked its ears.

Rita's expression was gentle as she shook her head. "I wouldn't do that, of course. Forgiving him isn't even an issue. He's my father now, and he's important to me. I'm grateful to him. If anything, it's my real father whom I can't forgive."

"Wha?"

"I didn't want him to choose death. It was selfish of him."

"Yes…"

It finally dawned on him—the reason why Rita had goaded

him to come out. She hadn't wanted to console him, nor had she wanted to cheer him up. She had wanted to tell him off, as his friend, for shutting her out and sulking by himself.

Less than five years had passed since then.

Gathered on the bookstore's rooftop, Mathias and the other leaders gazed across the lines of buildings stretching away. A cloth tarp pitched above them kept the piercing rays of the sun at bay. A constant breeze blew up from the river, rendering the location sufferable even at midday.

White smoke climbed towards the sky from all across town. The residents were preparing their meals. The food supply might have been limited, but Quinta's people still needed to eat, and anyone who assisted the Garrison received extra rations as a reward.

"That didn't lead to much," Klaus muttered wearily, perched on the edge of the roof.

He was an outlaw, one of a few Mathias had enlisted to help him escape Fuerth and travel back to Quinta. Short of stature, ill-natured, he had daggers for eyes. Ever since their first meeting, he had treated Mathias with disdain and never bothered to hide his misgivings. Yet Klaus was still with him, making common cause and even beginning to show a certain amount of trust.

"You mean Gabriele?" Mathias asked, still standing.

"Yeah. He didn't know anything of use. Just spent the whole

time racing from one place to the next."

"I suppose."

Mathias recalled their conversation from downstairs, earlier that morning. They had asked Gabriele about the exterior: about the other districts and villages, and whether he'd seen anything unusual or come across anybody who had the big picture.

Gabriele had sat himself among the mountains of stacked books and done little more than pout and whine.

"How should I know about the other districts? If I'd known how, I'd have gone to one ages ago. I didn't know my left from my right when that guy there picked me up. Klaus, I mean. And the other villages… Wiped out, all of them. Hardly surprising, eh? I came across a few survivors like me, but they were all on edge. It's a constant scramble, for food."

He'd even wanted to know why they were bothering to ask questions in the first place.

"If you really want to know, why not go look yourselves? You can get out."

To this Mathias had said, "True, we could use the Night Harvest, but there's a limit to the amount of ground we can cover before dawn. We can't move during daytime, not without a horse."

"Right, I guess it'd be over if a Titan spotted you."

"Exactly."

"Why do you have to do all the investigating, anyway? Surely it's the job of the officials. Them, or the military."

"I believe Klaus already mentioned this. The situation in Quinta is far from normal."

"A dictatorship, as they say. And what was it again…'reign of terror'?" Nikki tested her new vocabulary.

Like Klaus, she had belonged to the band of outlaws. While it was a little hard to gauge what she was thinking—mostly she looked as though she wasn't thinking at all—she had the ability, during critical moments, to keep a cool head and make the right decisions. She was also a master at picking locks and highly proficient with firearms.

Mathias spoke to "the young man from outside," Gabriele.

"Rita—the person currently ruling over Quinta—has lost all interest in the outside world. She won't send an envoy to the interior, nor will she survey the immediate vicinity. She simply runs the town as she sees fit."

And it was all because of him.

Half a year ago, enlisting a band of criminals on the condition that he'd hand over the precious artworks hidden in the courtyard of his family mansion, Mathias had left the refuge of Fuerth to return to Quinta. Yet on arrival, as they were getting ready to cart out the various items, they had been spotted by soldiers on patrol.

Rita had been among them.

Rita…

She was Mathias' childhood friend, the very person he had

come back for, the reason he had decided to cross the exterior and put himself in danger.

Now she ruled Quinta.

It was there at the mansion that the accident occurred. Mathias' gun fired. One of Rita's subordinates, a boy soldier, died, his head blown away. With nothing else to do Mathias fled the scene. He had never intended to kill the young boy, but that would mean nothing to Rita. Her transformation, and the current state of Quinta it had brought about, was all his fault.

This, at least, was how he saw it. Nikki said he was being overly self-conscious, but he couldn't shake the guilt.

It was the reason he'd founded the resistance movement. He couldn't look the other way. He had a duty to restore the town to more normal conditions.

He was fortunate in that he had a good many friends and acquaintances in Quinta. And many were dissatisfied with the current state of affairs.

The number of sympathizers had grown with each passing day, so that now over a hundred civilians were clandestine comrades. They worked together to canvass new members, united in the cause of bringing down Rita's regime.

It would be fastest to persuade Rita in person, but Mathias was sure she despised him with all her heart. He was a wanted criminal, and the posters on display across Quinta were marked "Dead or Alive." The moment he showed his face, far from talking any sense into her, he would be cut to pieces by blades designed to fell Titans.

Gabriele nodded, looking satisfied with Mathias' explanation. "So I've heard. And this woman is pretty young?" He'd been fanning his collar the entire time they'd been inside the bookstore, sending puffs of air into his clothes. He appeared to be from a village with a climate cooler than Quinta's.

"She is," Mathias admitted. "Under normal circumstances the royal government would never permit…a rank-and-file soldier's dictatorship. But the government hasn't sent anyone our way. We have no idea what's going on. And we have no means to convey our predicament."

"They've probably given up on you. Either that, or the interior districts have their hands full."

"And that's what we wanna find out," Nikki chimed in. She had been drinking ever since she'd arrived. She acted as carefree as always, but it was clear to Mathias that she drank more now than half a year ago. He was sure that, in her own way, she felt the same daily pressures and anxieties.

Mathias spoke to Gabriele again. "We did manage to send someone out, just once, and on horseback, to convey our situation. To the nearest interior district. But we've had no response."

"This person hasn't returned?"

"That's right."

"When are you talking about?"

"It was almost three months ago. Right when the Night Harvest first started."

"And you're sure this person didn't just settle on the other side? I mean, life in an interior town would be better than, you know, this?"

"He's not that kind of person."

The man who'd left for Fuerth, the next district towards the interior, was Jarratt. He was an enormous, muscle-bound old man, and he, too, had been part of Klaus and Nikki's band of outlaws.

"Perhaps we should move on to our reports, now?"

The voice of the bookstore's owner, Derek, pulled Mathias back to the present. He was a friend of Suzanne, Mathias' home tutor and one of their family servants. Mathias had often visited the store—the bookstore that stood beneath them now—when he was younger to buy certain books at her behest.

It was Derek whom Mathias had approached when he'd first formed the idea of setting up a resistance. While he'd only done so in the belief that Derek would at least not betray him, the aging proprietor turned out to have a great number of trustworthy friends—more specifically, friends who were "bibliophiles, anti-establishment by nature" who welcomed a resistance movement against the regime.

"Not that I have anything worth reporting, of course," Derek conceded.

"Nor do I," said Klaus.

"How's Bernhardt holding up?" Nikki asked Amanda, the fifth member of the resistance leadership in attendance.

She was the only one they had on the inside. Though she served as Rita's deputy, apparently they were the same rank. She was attractive, cold, and the one who had broken Mathias' arm four months earlier.

Early that morning, Mathias had been on his way to a meeting when Garrison soldiers had spotted him. They'd given chase, and he'd been cornered into a back alley. When he'd tried to resist arrest, Amanda had blithely snapped his arm. Yet, just as he thought he would be taken in, events took a surprising turn.

Confirming that she had no subordinates nearby, Amanda put her mouth up to his ear and told him she wanted to join the resistance.

Mathias of course feigned ignorance. She had just broken his best arm. The pain was excruciating, he'd come out in an oily sweat, and he had tears in his eyes. He doubted another man would have extended his trust under such circumstances.

Unruffled, and, without his asking, Amanda began to explain in great detail the state of the Garrison Regiment that controlled Quinta. That was when Mathias first learned Bernhardt was being kept alive.

Bernhardt.

He had been the outlaws' leader, that is to say, Klaus and

Nikki's boss. After Mathias accidentally shot and killed the boy soldier in Rita's retinue, Bernhardt alone had been captured. As a result, he had borne the full brunt of her rage.

At first he'd only been held in confinement, but since the Night Harvest began he was being sent outside solo and in handcuffs. While he'd once belonged to the Military Police Brigade, even he couldn't take on a Titan with his hands tied. And so he followed orders, harvesting through the night and returning to Quinta at dawn.

In this way, once every few days, Rita exposed him to the greatest possible terror and humiliation. That she didn't kill him, despite harboring such visceral resentment, probably reflected strategic thinking on her part: kept alive, he might serve to lure in Mathias and his friends.

Her thinking was spot on.

Klaus and Nikki had only joined the resistance to rescue Bernhardt. As wanted criminals, and with no network of their own in Quinta, they couldn't afford to shrug off Mathias' connections and knowledge.

"Just the same." Amanda outlined Bernhardt's situation to everyone present. "She sends him out to gather fruit, on separate days from the others so he's alone. Handcuffed."

"She's treating him like a dog," Klaus hissed.

"Worse, no?" Amanda continued impassively. "He gets practically no food at all. He's left to eat stuff raw when he's out gathering."

Nikki angled her head. "So, just vegetables and fruit?"

Amanda nodded. "I heard that he eats rats, too. Although I can't say for sure, as we haven't spoken in person."

Nikki grimaced and made a retching sound.

Amanda went on some more. "I only caught a brief glimpse from the top of the wall, but he looked like he'd lost a lot of weight. You might not even recognize him even if you ran into him."

"Can't you do something?" Nikki asked for the umpteenth time. "You are in the Garrison and all. Be great if you sneaked him out, ey?"

"If I could do that, I would have a long time ago. I'm not in charge of him, so I can't get close. I could put in to be reallocated, I suppose, but I'd come under suspicion. The girl doesn't trust me all that much."

The girl. Amanda was the only one there who referred to Rita that way.

"Then you shouldn't try," cautioned Mathias.

For the moment Amanda was their only contact on the inside. They couldn't risk losing her because of some ill-conceived plan.

Amanda pinched her eyes in disgust. "You know she keeps a tighter watch on him than she does on the food and drink. It's like he's some kind of prize."

It suggested how obsessed she'd become with him. That, in turn, suggested how obsessed she'd become with Mathias.

There was another powerful gust of wind. Mathias gazed out towards the wall enclosing the town. Cannons were spaced at regular intervals, with soldiers patrolling between them. Baking under the direct sunlight, they looked as miserable as one might expect.

Derek shuffled in his chair. "It would appear we have no choice, then, but to use the Night Harvest. Somebody leaves a day ahead, finds somewhere to spend the night, and contacts Bernhardt the next day. If we hand him the Vertical Maneuvering Equipment, can't he bring his helper back over the wall as well?"

Bernhardt had been in the Military Police Brigade. He was an expert with the Vertical Maneuvering Equipment. Even with both hands tied, he wouldn't find it a particular challenge to scale the wall with a couple of other people.

"If it was just getting through the night, maybe," Klaus said, looking and sounding grim. "The problem is that we'd have to last the day."

"Right," Mathias agreed. "Even if we're lucky and there is a harvest the day before, we'd still need to spend a full day outside. That's when the Titans are at their most active. If one found us, we'd be eaten alive. And they're naturally drawn to people."

"Whole day without a horse—might be kinda tough."

Nikki was leaning back in her chair, gazing up at the azure

sky. She was right. With a horse there was at least the possibility of escape, even if a Titan did spot you. On foot, escape was all but impossible.

Amanda's hand moved to her hip. Off duty and in plain civilian attire, she wasn't carrying any weapons. "I can secure the Vertical Maneuvering Equipment, but a horse is pushing it."

Nikki brought her head back forwards. "I'd be happy to go," she offered.

"It's a difficult decision," Mathias said, "but if we're doing this at all, we ought to go with people already familiar with the exterior. So Nikki, and—"

"Me, right?" Klaus turned to face them again.

"Yes. However, I can't help but imagine the worst-case scenario. Especially since Jarratt hasn't returned."

He was probably dead. If the worst happened and they ended up losing Klaus and Nikki too, the resistance's ability to fight would be significantly diminished.

"What if we practice using it a little?"

Amanda frowned at Nikki's proposal. "Practice using what?"

"The Vertical Maneuvering Equipment. We'd be taking it with us either way, right? To give to Bernhardt. If we learned how to use it, we might be able to get away even if a Titan did find us during the day. We could go up the wall, go up a big tree."

"You can't use the wall. The soldiers would definitely see you during the daytime."

Amanda knew every route the soldiers patrolled, along with the times of their shifts.

Derek modestly stated his own objection. "If you were seen they would shore up their guard, even supposing you weren't caught. We would lose all hope of rescuing Bernhardt."

"Plus," Amanda added, "it's extremely difficult for an amateur to hit a tree. You'd need three months of practice at least."

"Oh well, that's a shame," Nikki buckled and made a show of looking dejected.

Mathias got to his feet and said, "Let's wait and see just a little longer. Maybe something will change in the way they're guarding him."

"What if he dies in the meantime?" Klaus demanded. In other words, the more time they took, the greater the chances were of Bernhardt wasting away and expiring or becoming feed for a Titan.

"We need to hurry, of course. We do, but we want as many people on our side as possible if we're to take some concrete form of action."

"Right, canvassing." Klaus made a derisory snort. "You're sure that's not our main goal these days?"

"I'm sure."

The goal was to end Rita's stampede.

Try as he might, Mathias was unable to forget it.

***

For half a year, Rita's thoughts had been drifting back to one of two scenes.

The first was the instant of Duccio's murder. His head being blown apart, his body rising into the air, his falling slowly backwards.

Try as she might, she was unable to forget it.

The second had come a few days after his death, immediately after she'd interrogated the ex-MP.

"There's been a robbery! Close by. It…seems someone from your family was there when it happened, acting commander."

The moment the soldier finished his report, Rita raced out of the dungeon. She shot through the daylight streets—at full speed, using the Vertical Maneuvering Equipment. She must have reached the crime scene in under two minutes.

She saw her immediately. Her mother, Doris, was sprawled on the ground outside a bakery cafe.

"Mom!"

Rita ran to her as though possessed. Pushing the soldier helping Doris out of the way, she pulled her mother into her arms. Doris' face was covered in blood from her nose, itself broken and twisted. Her cheeks were swollen and one of her eyes was bruised shut. Her right leg was bent at an absurd angle.

She'd been there when the break-in had taken place. She'd

tried to talk the burglar down, he had lashed out in response, and she'd snapped her leg in the fall.

"Are you okay?!"

Doris opened her eyes a fraction. She struggled to open her mouth and string words together, but it was too much.

"Don't try to talk!"

"Acting commander. The burglar is still…"

Astoundingly, the criminal who had broken into the bakery cafe and violently attacked Doris was still holed up inside. One of the patrons had somehow managed to get Doris out.

"Just wait here, Mom."

Rita laid Doris back down and got to her feet. She entered the bakery cafe.

It was a small shop. There was a counter directly ahead, and behind it, shelves lined with stock. Four tables along the wall on the way in provided the only seating.

The burglar, a man, looked about thirty. His overgrown hair hung down awfully straight. He had retreated to the cafe's far-right corner, his arm around the neck of a young woman about Rita's own age. In his free hand he held a knife.

"Let her go," Rita commanded.

The man, covered in a repulsive amount of sweat, nevertheless appeared to be shivering. "The hell I will."

"Just let her go," Rita repeated.

He twitched his head in a shaking motion.

"I'm hungry. These guys are raking it in. I ain't doin' nothing wrong!"

"Okay, just—"

"I want food, and a horse. I'm getting the hell out of this place. I can't live like this!"

So selfish, thought Rita. *Thanks to people like him, the decent ones like Doris get hurt. Kids like Duccio end up dead.*

Her arm moved, her hand moved, unconsciously.

Rita's fingers squeezed the trigger and fired an anchor from one of the cylinders on her waist. The point ran straight through the man's chest. She heard him groan.

The girl he'd taken hostage began to scream.

Again, Rita's fingers moved unbidden. The Vertical Maneuvering Equipment started to wind in the anchor. It sped back terribly fast.

Without thinking Rita dropped into a crouch, planting her feet on the floor.

The man's body leapt and sliced through the air, sailing in towards Rita along with the anchor. The young woman was knocked to the ground.

His eyes were wide with disbelief. Half-mad with the pain in his chest, he swung his knife about frantically.

Rita unsheathed one of her blades. She simultaneously flicked the lever to free the anchor from the man's chest, averting a full-on collision. Just as the man passed before her eyes, she lifted her blade as if gliding it through the air. His throat ripped open.

Inertia sent the man tumbling into the floor even as blood fountained from his neck.

Everything felt like it was part of a dream.

"Acting commander..."

Rita realized some of her troops were standing there behind her. A crowd had formed outside the cafe, and a great number of civilians were peering through the entrance.

Until that moment, perhaps there had been a tendency among her subordinates to take her lightly. They had, in part, doubted her competence.

All that was gone. Not a fraction of uncertainty remained.

Instead, their eyes carried a look of fear. The same hue was present in the eyes of the civilians watching on at a remove.

I see, this is what I need.

If there are to be no more victims like Duccio and Doris.

Something had clicked, deep within her heart, like a lock coming undone. She heard the same sound every time the scenes replayed themselves in her mind.

***

It was night, two days after Gabriele's addition to the organization, and Mathias was walking through downtown with Nikki. They were on their way to visit Rita's mother, Doris.

Although she still lived in the same house, word was that she was like an empty shell.

It was only to be expected.

Her husband Henning, Rita's father, had been executed only a few months ago on charges of selling potions to help people kill themselves. Specifically, his torso had been devoured by "the plaza Titan" as per his daughter's directive.

Faced with such circumstances, no wife or mother could remain her former self.

Apparently, Rita and Doris no longer saw each other.

That, Mathias supposed, was true for him too.

His association with Rita's family dated back to his childhood. He and Doris had been close, and he knew Rita was perfectly aware that he might pay her mother a visit. Quite possibly she'd assigned someone to keep an eye on the place. If he approached carelessly, there was a high risk of being arrested and dragged out before Rita.

But he needed to talk to Doris in person, even just for five minutes, even just one, and even if it meant putting himself in danger. He needed to tell her that he intended to take a stand against her daughter.

The amount of people in the streets seemed mostly unchanged from before the fall of Wall Maria. The mood, however, was far darker. The streets and alleys overflowed with an almost tangible sense of fear and suspicion.

When they were about three blocks away from Doris' house, someone shouted, "Fire!"

Mathias and Nikki glanced at each other in silence. There indeed was an ashy smell in the air. Not long after they noticed this, the sky began to turn orange behind the rooftops of the buildings to their right. Something resembling black smoke climbed into the sky. Although fires were less frequent these days, they still broke out occasionally.

As it was relatively early, many residents were still awake. Windows overhead flung open in quick succession. People looked out with concerned faces from their front doors.

"Suits us nicely," Nikki said without stopping. "If there are any guards, this should distract them."

"Agreed."

Together, they began to approach Doris' home. The first floor had once housed Henning's apothecary, but the business had been shuttered since his execution.

Nikki crouched in towards the front door. Out of her jacket she produced a collection of metallic rods, each a different thickness and length. She'd use her vaunted lock-picking skills to get them in quickly. Calling Doris from outside and waiting for her to react would waste too much time.

"There we go!"

In a mere twenty seconds, Nikki was back on her feet and returning her tools to her pocket.

"Impressive, as always."

Nikki registered the praise with a satisfied chuckle.

The two of them hurried inside.

"Doris?" Mathias tried calling her name, quietly, but there was no response.

They continued in, carefully in case soldiers were waiting for them. With no source of illumination, it was almost totally dark. It didn't matter as Mathias knew his way around even with his eyes closed.

"Doris, we're coming in."

They crossed the apothecary and walked behind the counter. Opening the door, Mathias placed a foot on the stairs. He ascended them without seeing them. The faint outline of things came into view as he approached the second floor. Nikki followed soundlessly after him.

"It's Mathias. I'm sorry to barge in like this."

After trying again he proceeded to the far end of the second-floor corridor. Not that the building was all that large.

He saw her the moment he entered the street-side kitchen and dining room.

Doris was sitting in a chair she'd placed next to the window and staring blankly through it. She had been a strong and dynamic woman—now she'd lost a lot of weight, giving her a shrunken appearance. The flames of the fire outside colored one side of her face orange and cast deep shadows, accentuating her sunken cheeks.

"Doris," Mathias said again, his voice still subdued.

He wondered at first if she hadn't heard. Then, slowly, at her own pace, she began to turn around. Her eyes paused when she saw him, and drew into focus.

Anxiety began to swell in Mathias' chest. Had she lost her senses completely? He was unsure whether he ought to approach her.

But before he could decide what to do, Doris whispered, "You...came..."

Her voice had been barely louder than a mosquito, but its tone was enough to assure Mathias she was of sound mind. With his fears dispelled, he felt a flush of warmth come over him. Doris might have changed in appearance, but in essence she hadn't one bit.

"Yes. I came."

It was the first time they'd spoken in half a year. Only now did Mathias realize just how much he'd needed to see her. He found himself hurrying across the room. Doris, too, quickly got up from her chair. They fell into an embrace.

It felt perfectly natural.

Doris' head only came up to Mathias' shoulders. He'd always imagined her as a taller woman. The smell on her neck, on her hair and clothes, was one he knew well. It was similar to Rita's, but different too. Come to think of it, the house itself carried a familiar smell, reminiscent of Rita's. How had he failed to notice it until now?

Mathias was filled with sorrow. He took a series of deep breaths. He had to in order not to burst into tears with Nikki standing there behind him.

Right, Nikki.

Softly, carefully, as though handling a fragile object, Mathias held Doris out to arm's length. He glanced over his shoulder, indicating with a look the outlaw-turned-comrade.

"This is Nikki. She's a friend."

"Okay." Doris' voice was still hushed, but it was firm. She looked past Mathias and made a slight bow. "You're welcome here."

"Nice to meet you," Nikki reciprocated with some manners.

Doris returned her gaze to Mathias. "And, how are things?"

Mathias guessed she wasn't inquiring after his health. "How much do you know?" he asked back.

"It's hard to say. But I think I know most of what's happening. I often just sit and do nothing, these days. I have friends who visit and take care of me, though, and I hear lots of gossip that way. I do get the order of things mixed up every now and then." She glanced at the middle of the room. "Look at me, keeping you both on your feet. Take a seat. I'll go put on some tea."

"Thanks, but we can't stay long."

"Don't be silly." Doris crossed the room, dragging her right leg as she headed into the kitchen.

"Right, your leg!"

Mathias remembered then. Not long after Quinta got cut off, some burglar or bag-snatcher had assaulted Doris, and she'd fallen and broken her leg.

"Are you okay? Really, please—"

"Shush!"

Her voice was regaining some of its former buoyancy. Her deflated frame seemed a little larger. Mathias swapped glances with Nikki, before walking, still hesitant, up to the table.

"I'm so sorry about what happened to Henning," he said, facing the kitchen as he pulled himself a chair and took a seat.

Perhaps he shouldn't have reminded her of it. But he couldn't not mention it. Mathias knew that seeing his face would have transported Doris' thoughts back to Rita and Henning.

"Forgive me. I know condolences fall far short of what happened. I just…don't know what else to say."

"It's fine. Whatever you say, nothing can change what's done."

"I am sorry. Really."

"What do you have to apologize for?" Doris came back with a set of ceramic mugs and a bottle of liquor. "Sorry, seems this is all I've got. I assume it'll do?"

"Fantastic!" Nikki said.

This girl's a bonafide alcoholic, thought Mathias, but he nodded at Doris, who poured the liquor into three mugs before joining them at the table.

"I need to apologize because," he said, getting back to the subject, "I was the one who made Rita the way she is. I killed one of her soldiers… It was an accident, but that doesn't mean anything from her point of view."

"I'd thought as much."

"Sorry?"

"That it was an accident. He said the same thing, you know." She meant Henning, of course. Doris continued, "I'm sure the accident was a part of what caused this, but it wasn't everything. There's this too." She indicated her leg with her eyes. "In fact, this was probably the main cause. If I hadn't been so stupid…well, anyway. What I'm trying to tell you is that a number of things had to come together to make Rita snap the way she did."

Doris was holding her mug in both hands and gazing at the surface of the liquid. Mathias remembered when the four of them had gathered here to toast Rita's admission to the Garrison Regiment.

He could no longer recall how the liquor had tasted.

"Even if what I did isn't the sole cause…" Mathias lifted his mug. "As Rita's friend, I want to stop her. She believes she's building a utopia, but the way things are now is wrong whichever way you look at it."

"Yes. I think so too." Doris gave Nikki a quick look. "I heard that you're building a movement?"

"Wow...you really are on top of things."

"What are you planning to do? Specifically. It's okay, you don't have to tell me if you can't."

"We're not sure yet. But it looks like things will get a little rough."

"Of course. Otherwise you wouldn't be bringing people in."

"I'll have to stand up to Rita...I might even have to hurt her. Physically, and mentally. Of course, it's likely I'll be the one who gets covered in bruises."

"Yes, that's what I'm worried about." Doris smiled, although the smile didn't reach her eyes. It was a wry smile.

"Do I have your permission?" Mathias asked.

"To do what? To teach the girl a lesson?"

"Yes."

"Absolutely. It's clear this is hard on you, too. You'd find it much easier to leave her be."

"I still don't know if it's right. I'm still wavering."

"Why?"

Doris looked up from her liquor. Mathias saw that Nikki was also staring right at him as though to ask why he was still voicing such feelings.

I know. I still lack the nerve. But...

"I wonder if it won't make me the same as her. To hurt someone I care about, just because I happen to believe I'm right." He knew Rita wouldn't have executed Henning on a whim. She wasn't simply feeding people to the Titan.

"You're wrong," Doris flatly contradicted. "She had influence, she had standing. From the start of all this."

She turned to look out of the window. The fire appeared to be under control, and the sky was once again turning deep blue. Doris seemed to have noticed the change.

She left her seat, then re-emerged from the kitchen with a candle in hand, dragging her right leg.

"That wasn't the case with you. You started with nothing. You expressed your views and people came to join you. You never forced anyone into anything. It's completely different."

"I hope you're right."

"Believe in yourself." She lifted her drink. "Just don't do anything..." She broke off, sighing as she reconsidered her words. "To hell with it—be as reckless as you want."

"Thank you."

It had been worth coming here. A smile found its way to Mathias' face.

"I think I'm getting better at that."

"At being reckless?"

"Yes."

He got to his feet.

Nikki snatched what was left of the bottle as they were leaving.

The Harsh Mistress of the City

It was Mathias' fourth time on the Night Harvest.

The first had been soon after he'd sent Jarratt to Fuerth. Wanting to bring as many people into the resistance as possible, Mathias had taken the lead and fashioned himself a false identity to venture out into the dangerous night of the ex-interior. Luckily he'd convinced a number of people to join, and ever since it had become customary within the movement to use the Night Harvest to canvass new members.

Klaus and Nikki had recently volunteered themselves, claiming it suited them better than other duties.

"This is making me nervous," Mathias muttered, checking the condition of his right arm. The doctor had removed the splint, saying it was fully healed, but it still felt wrong somehow.

They were standing in line, watched over by young troops, who all bore a vague similarity to the boy soldier Mathias had killed. The dusk glow still lingered in the sky. Once the sun set, the gate would be hauled open, and they would be expelled from the confines of Quinta. Numerous watch fires already burned around the gate.

"Aren't you supposed to be used to this?" Gabriele said, looking up. He was a tad shorter than Mathias, but fairly muscular, no doubt due to six months of scrambling through the exterior.

"I wouldn't go that far."

"What, you leave all the dangerous work to your lackeys?"

"I'm a lackey too. I started the resistance, that's all."

"Right, you're the founder…" Gabriele folded his arms and studied Mathias.

"Although," Mathias added, "it's a fact that I've left the dangerous work to others. Precisely why I decided to come this time."

Only a few days earlier, Gabriele had revealed some unexpected information. Although he had lost his horse just before arriving in Quinta, luckily he'd found a fissure in the face of a cliff and spent the daytime hiding inside.

A commotion had broken out among the members of the resistance.

They could leave Quinta with the Night Harvest, spend the day inside the hole, then rendezvous with Bernhardt. They could deliver the Vertical Maneuvering Equipment without braving a Titan attack.

It would be a dangerous gamble.

Mathias had given the go-ahead to the plan, even volunteering to execute it in person. He had to be the one to tell Bernhardt about the resistance and Quinta's status quo. Derek had objected, but Mathias believed Bernhardt might refuse to cooperate if the rundown came from anyone else.

There was shouting from the front, and slowly, the gate began to open.

"Looks like we're off."

Prompted by Gabriele, Mathias trudged forth with the rest of the despairing civilians. There was a faint warmth as he passed by the watch fires. The dancing flames cast faint shadows of Mathias and the crowd onto the wall and the ground.

They proceeded toward the wall that parted the world of men from a world that was not theirs. By the exit, soldiers were handing out old boxes and baskets. Tonight's destination was, once again, the abandoned orchard. The ripe fruit was easy to pluck from the trees by hand, without any special tools. Mathias and Gabriele patiently awaited their turn, then took one basket to share between them. The wicker looked splintered, broken enough to cut skin.

A woman approached from the direction of the street. She pushed her way through the people in line and pulled Mathias into a close hug.

It was Jodi. A teacher and one of the resistance's earliest members, she was ten or so years older than Mathias but somehow still smacked of a girl.

"Be careful out there."

She placed a hand on Mathias' back and looked up with tears in her eyes. *A convincing act?* No, she seemed to mean it. Mathias felt a surge of genuine gratitude. Similar exchanges were happening around them. Husbands and wives, lovers, parents and children, all hugging and whispering.

The soldiers refrained from ordering them apart.

Jodi was dressed in baggier clothes than usual. The temperature dropped overnight and leading up to the morning, so

Mathias and Gabriele wore thick overcoats as well.

Pretending to return the embrace, Mathias transferred the cloth bag hidden under her garments to the inside of his own coat. The bag contained the Vertical Maneuvering Equipment.

When his hand brushed over her hip, he couldn't help but blush. He was glad his surroundings were dark.

The Vertical Maneuvering Equipment was made up of the wire-reeling machine, cylinders of compressed gas, and the anchors and their firing mechanism. It weighed its worth, but not so much that it couldn't be carried in one hand. Since the system was designed to enable aerial combat, it was manufactured to be as light as possible. The blades used to slay Titans, meanwhile, were too bulky and had been left behind.

Jodi handed Mathias another package, this one the size of an adult's forearm. Inside was a shotgun wrapped in cloth along with a belt to fix it on his leg. It wasn't exactly the same kind as the weapon that slew Rita's subordinate but was similar enough. It was the last thing Mathias wanted with him. At the same time, he couldn't very well leave Quinta unarmed.

Jodi took a step back after confirming the success of the handover.

Double-checking, Mathias asked, "So, nothing's changed?"

"Bernhardt's scheduled for tomorrow. The same venue as tonight's."

They had been painstaking with their choice of day for the

operation. It would all come to nothing if Bernhardt's Night Harvest didn't directly follow that of the residents at large. Jodi moved away, letting the crowd carry her towards the edge of the column.

"Bit plain, that one," Gabriele commented, watching out of the corner of his eye as she left.

"She's a good person."

"Not my type."

They crossed the passageway from the interior and were ejected with the rest of the civilians into the world outside.

The smell of the air changed. By now the odor of smoldering wood and the stink of putrefied corpses were long gone. Yet the air still felt as though it carried something offensive that cloyed on their hair and skin.

Under his clothes, Mathias slung his bag's belt over his shoulder. The bag itself he swung around to the front. Gabriele was carrying the basket, which now contained the wrapped shotgun.

They kept pace with the others, who were visibly jumpy, no doubt beside themselves with fear, given that a Titan could attack them at any moment.

They reached the orchard after an hour of hiking through woodland. There they split into teams designated by the military and began the harvesting process. They were all careful not to leave too much space between themselves and the others.

Mathias and Gabriele slipped away from the ring of people,

acting as though they were only going to take a leak.

Mathias stopped at the orchard's boundary and accepted the package containing the shotgun from Gabriele. He unwrapped the weapon and studied it. He knew he'd never warm to this type of firearm. He would have preferred to entrust it to Gabriele, but the latter said he didn't know how to use it. "You could show me," he said airily, but Mathias hardly felt like it.

Despite his distaste, he used the belt to fix the barrel of the weapon to his right leg. His right arm was still below par, but it was his best bet if he needed to handle the thing.

He raised his head and looked around.

"Think you can find it from here?"

Before them was a grassy plain, with only the occasional tree. The terrain was bathed in faint light, and to Mathias every direction looked the same, but Gabriele responded with a firm nod.

"Yeah. Lucky the sky is clear."

He began to walk, taking confident steps. In no time at all they reached a stream. They continued along the bank for close to two hours.

"This is it."

Gabriele stopped and jerked his chin ahead. A sheer cliff face stood just as he had described, rising up behind a dense growth of trees. It was ten meters high at the most. From the perspective of someone used to a fifty-meter wall, it didn't feel particularly big. The surface was cracked, yielding a gap about thirty centimeters wide.

"Wow, I see."

Mathias advanced and put a hand against the rock near the entrance. The hard surface appeared to continue all the way inside and up to the top of the cliff itself. It was far deeper than Mathias had imagined.

They camped outside the fissure until shortly before dawn, then relieved their bladders and finally shuffled inside.

Gabriele went in first, leaving Mathias closer to the opening. Once inside it was almost impossible to move.

It took less than an hour for the discomfort to become unbearable.

"What can I say? They move quieter than you'd expect. There could be one out there right now. You could be snapped up the moment you stick your head out."

"Right," Mathias accepted.

While he understood this, it didn't help alleviate his torment. At least he was able to lean into the surfaces in front and behind of him, but only a year ago, he could never have pictured himself spending half a day on his feet in such a cramped space.

He drank as little as possible to minimize the need to urinate. Just once, unable to hold it in any longer, he risked his life to run out and heed nature's call.

The narrowness of the fissure meant they were only exposed

to direct sunlight from above for a few dozen minutes. Mathias had kept his overcoat over his head for the duration and sweltered underneath. Snacking occasionally on cured meat, and feeling dizzy, somehow he managed to last until sunset.

"That should do it."

Mathias experienced a heartfelt sense of relief when Gabriele uttered the words.

Squeezing out from the gap, he started to work the kinks from his body.

He couldn't see any Titans. He couldn't hear breathing or footsteps. For the second night in a row, the sky was free of clouds and the moon's shape distinct.

"Shall we?" Mathias finally said.

"Uh huh."

They traced their previous route in reverse, trampling over tall grass.

"What did you say this guy's name was?"

"Bernhardt."

"Right. You must value him, going to all this trouble."

"I'm not sure that's the right word."

Without Bernhardt, Mathias would have never made it to Quinta. And yet, if they had never struck their deal, neither would he have ended up killing Rita's subordinate.

She would never have broken—he felt that was the right word—and Quinta's fate would have been significantly different.

Mathias couldn't summarize his feelings for Bernhardt in a single word, but at any rate, the man was an excellent fighter.

He'd served with the Military Police Brigade. He was adept at wielding the Vertical Maneuvering Equipment and those special blades.

He could kill Titans.

"No, you're right. He is valuable."

"Can't say you look like you want to see him."

"But I do." There was work for Bernhardt to do.

"So how do we find him?"

"We'll have to cover as much ground as we can." The orchard was fairly expansive, and there was always the chance of Bernhardt's itinerary having changed during the course of the day. "If we have to we can wait near the gate at dawn and meet up with him that way."

"Except the soldiers would see us."

"If they do...we'll probably have to distance ourselves from Quinta for a bit. They'll be on alert, so it'll be hard to get back over the wall, even with Bernhardt."

"So worst case, we rough it out here for a few more days. Well, I'm used to that."

Mathias remembered his excruciating day. He doubted Bernhardt would choose to go through something like that. No, Bernhardt—at least, the Bernhardt of old—would find it simpler to "dispose of some inexperienced soldiers" and go back over the

He needed to run fast. But he couldn't trip. If he fell, even just once, he didn't think he could stand up again.

Gabriele was moving easily through the trees. His legs stayed clear of swollen roots, fallen trunks, and jutting rocks. He could have been running on a paved road in the middle of the day.

There was a sound like a cannon booming.

The ground shook, throwing Mathias into the air a fraction. He lurched forwards and almost toppled. Regaining his balance at the last moment, he grabbed his windmilling bag with both hands and turned to look back.

"It's coming!"

The Titan was crawling on all fours. The crashing noise had been from its hands pounding into the ground. Its huge face, looming higher than their heads, still looked sunken in sorrow. Its brow furrowed, its teeth clamped together, it looked like it was ready to burst into tears.

Why it didn't chase them on its feet was anyone's guess. There was no point in trying to divine the reason behind an aberrant Titan's behavior. All that could be said for sure was that it wanted to eat them alive.

It kept coming, its hands and knees causing the earth to shake. It was moving notably faster than Mathias or Gabriele. Yet it was, of course, much larger, and the woods were quite dense here. Time and time again the trees frustrated the Titan's progress, the countless trunks acting as obstacles.

Its arms shooting between trees and snatching at Mathias and Gabriele, its face ever sorrowful, the Titan looked like a prisoner appealing for mercy through the bars of a cell.

In truth, Mathias and Gabriele were the ones who could use some mercy.

"Focus, damn it!" Gabriele yelled. "Gun! You've got a gun, right? Use it!"

Mathias remembered with a start. The accursed shotgun. The root evil. What a bitter irony that he was now dependent on it for his life. He felt around his right thigh.

No good. He wasn't going to make it in time. He'd be Titan feed before he could pull it free and fire.

He kicked the ground as hard as he could, leaping to the left. An oversized jaw shot past the spot he'd been in only a moment earlier. Rows of teeth came together with a bone-rattling snap.

Then came the impact—the Titan's shoulder had knocked him into the air.

"Hey?!"

The pain registered at the same moment as Gabriele's call.

There was a second rush of pain. He'd come down and hit the earth hard. The moment he realized he was about to pass out, he experienced a sudden jolt of clarity.

I keep my eyes open or I die.

There was a tree next to him. He used the bark for support and pulled himself upright.

He felt lighter.

Why?

"Uh oh…" The bag with the Vertical Maneuvering Equipment was gone. The belt had snapped, either when he'd been thrown into the air or when he'd landed. "Where is it?!"

He quickly scanned the area around him. His vision was gradually clearing.

"There!"

Part of the bag was poking from the undergrowth. Even at a glance he could see it was covered in dirt. He prayed the contents were intact.

He summoned all his speed to race to it.

"Above you!"

Mathias looked up in response to the warning.

The Titan's face was coming in. The gigantic mouth opened, ready to bite at him from diagonally above.

"I can't…" *die yet.*

But his legs wouldn't listen, neither halting nor swerving from their course.

He swallowed. His upper body felt like it might work.

The Titan was farther away than the last time.

Mathias' right hand fumbled around his thigh and pulled the shotgun free. He used his left hand to set the mechanism, readying it to fire, then brought the same hand up to steady the barrel.

His whole body registered the heat of the Titan's breath. It was strangely odorless. If anything it smelled like nature, verdant, like the grass and trees of the forest.

Mathias angled his arm upwards.

He took aim at the deep end of the cavernous opening and pulled the trigger.

There was a spark as the gunpowder detonated and cast the area in momentary daylight. Countless pellets fired from the weapon. With the recoil, it felt as though Mathias' whole arm had exploded.

Overwhelmed by the discharge of sound and the sudden flash, this time his eyes did go dark, and his ears silent.

He staggered backwards, dropped the weapon, and tumbled onto his backside.

Gradually, his vision and hearing returned. An image began to form under the moonlight.

The skin on the Titan's face was torn to shreds. Chunks of flesh, spattered everywhere, gushed hot steam. Without so much as moaning, the Titan ducked its vaporous head and slowly shook it side to side.

"The river!"

Gabriele was shouting. His voice sounded awfully distant. Mathias couldn't decide if Gabriele was genuinely far away or if it was the ringing in his ears.

"The river…"

"It's close by, I can hear it! Jump in before it gets you. You can use it to get away!"

"Ah…"

It *was* difficult to picture a Titan wading into water. And if the current was fast enough, the river would carry him free in no time.

"This way!"

"Okay."

Mathias managed to get to his feet. He was surprised to note that his right arm wasn't broken. Everything seemed to be working. He could flex his fingers without difficulty.

He began to move in the direction of Gabriele's voice, but turned sharply around to snatch up the bag that had fallen to the ground.

The Titan continued to shake its head. The motion was slower now, less conspicuous. The steam was beginning to dissipate, too. Eyes and a nose were already coming into view. The creature's lips, decimated just moments earlier, were also regaining their shine and suppleness.

Titans possessed extraordinary powers of regeneration.

Mathias began to run again.

The sound of his own breathing grated on him. The explosive sound of the shotgun still rang in his ears. But despite this he could make out the faint sound of running water. He had to be moving in the right direction.

He pushed his way through a leafy patch of thin branches.

The dark fell abruptly away. Mathias wondered if there had been another explosion. A silent explosion.

But no—he'd simply come out into the open.

A broad stream flowed in front of him. A tributary, he supposed, of the great river that connected the districts, it had to be thirty meters wide.

The surface reflected the night sky, and for a moment Mathias had the illusion that two moons were out.

More woodland stretched away from the bank on the far side.

The ground rumbled again. All of the trees around him began to sway.

Mathias looked back over his shoulder.

A giant, sorrowful face was encroaching into the moonlight. The rays fell on its nose, its cheeks, its jaw, its eyebrows—

Mathias jumped before he saw any more.

Wheeling his limbs in the air, he tried to hit the surface as far from the bank as he could.

He was overtaken by an almost painful cold.

Confusion. He thrashed desperately in the water, afraid of drowning. The bag was getting in the way. Yet it was the presence of the same that helped him regain his composure.

He needed to deliver it to Bernhardt.

They needed to return over the wall, together.

He could hold his breath for a while. People didn't die so

easily.

Forcing his tense body to relax, but taking firm hold of the bag, Mathias gave himself to the current.

Still underwater, he opened his eyes. Visibility was better than he'd expected. The water seemed roughly as deep as he was tall.

A multitude of bubbles escaped upwards. It felt like being inside a cloud of white vapor, the steam that erupted from a Titan's wounds.

The current was faster than it had appeared above the surface. Mathias could feel himself being carried away like driftwood.

I can make it, the Titan won't get to me now.

As soon as the relief hit him, he heard a loud dull sound. A sudden rush of water shoved him forwards and carried him farther downstream.

Mathias' disorientation reached its peak.

The current swept him around to face upstream. The water was dark and cloudy. Bubbles mixed with dirt, blocking the view completely. As this began to clear…

Impossible.

…the Titan's face appeared from inside.

Its sorrowful eyes were trained firmly on Mathias. Prone in the river, "shallow" for its huge frame, the Titan stretched its arms forwards, flattened its palms, and drove the water backwards on either side.

It closed the distance between them in a mere moment. Before Mathias knew it, the creature's nose was there before his eyes, close enough to touch.

The Titan flexed its shoulder muscles. By the time Mathias glimpsed this, its hands were already closing in on either side. With a motion similar to when it had parted water, the Titan clamped its hands around Mathias' torso.

He gagged from the pressure.

The Titan came up so it was free of the current from the waist upwards. Mathias was wrenched out of the river.

He tried to breathe but ended up swallowing water and retched violently. Fine particles of sand clogged up his mouth and nose. He lifted his face, his breathing ragged.

Moonlight shone over the Titan. From the drenched hair clinging to its sorrowful features water cascaded down to its shoulders.

"Ahh…." *I didn't make it. So, what, Titans can swim?*

He could think of nothing more. There was no reliving of old memories. There was only the staggering awe of the sight before him.

Out of nowhere something landed on the creature's immense shoulder.

It was about the size of a person.

No, it *was* a person. A man, tall and shockingly thin.

Backhanding some sort of pole, he brandished it high above

his head. As he did, the Titan turned its head to look at him. The man brought the object down, stabbing it deep into the Titan's eye.

Its head jerked backwards. A huge cloud of steam gushed out of the socket, and the hands holding Mathias dipped. He was pulled back into the river, and water rushed into his nostrils and mouth again. He shook his head and struggled, desperate for fresh air.

The Titan's grip eased a little. Mathias squirmed, and his face just barely broke the surface. The man from before kicked off the Titan's shoulder, took lightly to the air, and fell out of Mathias' line of sight.

The Titan's hands opened fully. Once again, Mathias' head dipped back into the stream. He needed to get away but couldn't summon the strength.

He floated to the surface and began drifting.

There was an almighty crash of water, and a huge wave rolled into him. Apparently the Titan had collapsed into the stream and was thrashing. Mathias kept sinking and resurfacing. His vision began to blur, then to turn black. He couldn't hear anything. His senses were failing.

That man. The man just now…

He had the sense that time had passed—a second, a day, even a whole year. The world slowly regained its colors, sounds, and smells.

There was pressure around his upper body. Did the Titan have him again?

There was the sound of water, and of heavy breathing mixed with it.

The pressure and sound receded.

Then, his chest felt constricted yet again. He was being tugged at his shoulder and by the collar behind his neck.

He was hauled upward and tossed into the air; he felt the coldness of the wind, he crashed into grass and root, and he rolled over on the ground, facing up at—

"Well, well, look who we've got here," a familiar voice came from above.

Mathias blinked. It seemed as though someone, most likely the man who'd launched the surprise attack on the Titan, had grabbed him and pulled him clear of the stream. Whoever he was, he was standing with his hands folded over his stomach and peering down into Mathias' face. Water dripped from the extremities of his overgrown hair and beard.

"A coincidence indeed!"

The image came finally into focus: Bernhardt, standing in the light of the moon and grinning ferociously.

"Bernhardt..." No other words came out.

The man's voice was the same, but his appearance was utterly transformed. It was just as Amanda had said. He was so scrawny he looked like a different person. His hair and beard were overgrown, and while he had always looked stylish, he was now wrapped in what looked like dirty rags thrown together around the waist and shoulders. And yet his skin was clean. He must have been using the Night Harvests to cleanse himself.

His wrists were locked in black, heavy-looking metal restraints. The iron rings were joined by a chain no longer than twenty centimeters. Had he launched his surprise attack on the Titan and hauled Mathias out of the tributary despite such a handicap?

He was still monstrously good then.

"My, how you've changed!" Bernhardt said, proffering his hand.

Mathias had been in this situation before. In the tavern, where he'd almost been killed.

Still saving my life, Mathias thought sourly.

"I didn't expect to see you, certainly not out here. Is it visiting time?"

"Pretty much."

This time, Mathias didn't hesitate to take Bernhardt's hand. His own arm felt heavy.

He let Bernhardt pull him up. In the process the bag, which he'd hugged to his side unbeknownst to himself, fell to the ground and let loose its prize. Mathias was amazed. Plunging into a stream, swept away by its current, and snatched up by a

Titan, he nonetheless hadn't let go of the bag.

Bernhardt saw it immediately. "A-ha!" he said, sounding delighted. "More than just a visit it seems."

"I thought I'd bring a gift."

Mathias released Bernhardt's hand and bent down to the ground. He held up the Vertical Maneuvering Equipment, soaked and covered in dirt, for Bernhardt to see.

The outlaw's eyes stretched wide. "I would expect no less from the scion of a merchant association. You understand a prisoner's wants and needs."

"I'm no such thing, not anymore."

"So it seems!"

Bernhardt examined Mathias from head to toe, then laughed with genuine pleasure.

It was true that Mathias' appearance had changed drastically. His hair was shorter, his cheeks were covered in stubble, and he wore clothes that were spartan to the extreme. For the last six months, if only for the most part as a practical measure to evade Rita's pursuit, he had led an austere life.

"Here."

Mathias held out the Vertical Maneuvering Equipment. Bernhardt took it with such loving care it could have been a newborn child. He stroked its casing.

Behind him was the tributary, its surface covered in a blanket of steam. It was as though the water had vaporized. The Titan lay supine in it, tossing, turning, drawing away. The damage to its face was already partially healed, but whenever it tried to stand the current robbed it of its foothold.

There was something comical about the scene, although Mathias wouldn't have seen it that way had the creature been even ten meters closer.

"Hey, are you okay?!"

Gabriele jumped into sight, parting his way through the undergrowth. He took in Mathias and Bernhardt in turn, then blinked rapidly.

Bernhardt raised an eyebrow and gave Mathias an inquiring look. "Who is this character?"

How best to describe Gabriele? "A new friend. He helped get me this far."

"A-ha."

"He's familiar with the situation outside."

"Come on, old man, get a move on!"

"Hm." With deft movements Bernhardt unfastened the Vertical Maneuvering Equipment's belt and slung it around his waist. "He does have a point. I recommend we find somewhere else to chat."

"Oh. So you're the guy…" Gabriele finally seemed to realize that the man standing before him was the entire reason they were out here in the first place.

Bernhardt gave a satisfied smile and made quick work of

donning the Vertical Maneuvering Equipment. The levers that fired the anchors and controlled the wires were normally placed on either side of the waist, but Bernhardt had opted to put them both on his left. This was no doubt so he could operate them simultaneously even with his restraints.

"Can't you get them off?" Mathias asked, glancing at them.

Bernhardt gave him a dreary look and held up his arms and gave the chain a rattle. "I did try a few times, but these need more than rocks to break them. No, I'm afraid they need the attention of a professional—a blacksmith, or a weapon maker."

"Right..."

"But that's by the by. There's a place I'd like to show you. Follow me."

With that, Bernhardt took point and started to walk.

After crossing the woods and climbing a low hill, they reached an area where small huts huddled next to each other.

It was an abandoned settlement. There were no corpses, and no signs that there had ever been any. The residents must have evacuated as soon as they'd heard of Wall Maria's fate.

"Not too shabby, right?"

Bernhardt led them to an open space, the settlement's square. There, a single chair was set up next to a well.

"If you'd allow me a moment."

Bernhardt entered a nearby hut and came back out with two

similar chairs.

He had something else tucked under his arm.

The restraints were still locked to his wrists. Earlier, the three of them together had tried to get them off, but to no avail.

"Can I help?" Mathias offered.

"No no, you're guests here." Bernhardt arranged the chairs around the well, sat on the rightmost, the one that had been there first, and held aloft the other object. It was a bottle, half-full with some kind of liquid. "Booze. The inhabitants here were a considerate bunch. They took the trouble of leaving this behind for me." He popped the cork and took a mouthful.

Translated, he'd appropriated it from one of the empty houses, but Mathias decided not to object.

Bernhardt offered them the bottle. "How about some?"

"No, thank you." Mathias shook his head, still standing. He needed to stay sharp. "We are outside the wall, you realize?"

"A wise decision."

"Me, I'll have some."

Plonking himself down next to Bernhardt, Gabriele took the bottle and held it to his mouth. He took a few noisy swigs, then wiped the dregs with his sleeve and let out a satisfied sigh, all of it rather theatrically. Mathias shook his head, appalled, then took the seat on the far left.

It was quiet.

Mathias leaned back into his chair and saw the blue-tinged

night sky spread out above them. He was nearly lulled into thinking the spot peaceful and secure.

Offering back the bottle to Bernhardt, Gabriele said, "You're a fun guy, old man. You've got more fire than most people inside the wall."

They had completed their introductions on the way. Gabriele, for his part, appeared genuinely dazzled by the skill Bernhardt had displayed in ridding them of the Titan.

Bernhardt took the bottle. "Not so! Just look at me. I trust you are aware of my present circumstances?"

"Yeah, more or less."

"Once every three days or so, I am sent out on the Night Harvest. The soldiers tell me to return with a full crate. Alas, I find it hard to muster the enthusiasm." He let his eyes drop to the bottle in his hands. "I like to slack off, much as we're doing right now. As a result they punish me, and I never see anything of food. I haven't a flicker of fire left in me."

"Yeah, right!" Gabriele snorted, cracking up. "I doubt you'd be up to blinding Titans if that was true."

"Just good luck, my friend. Besides, I'm a kind-natured soul." Bernhardt put on a broad smile, watching Mathias as he passed the bottle back to Gabriele. "I find myself oddly capable when I need to aid the needy."

"Is that kind-natured or more like, I don't know, weird?"

The two of them seemed to get along preternaturally well.

Perhaps it was because they were both thorough optimists.

And I'm the opposite, thoroughly sullen, Mathias derided himself. Even so, he couldn't refrain from posing the question.

"Do you hold it against me?"

"You're not asking me, are you?" Bernhardt affected astonishment, stretching his eyes wide open.

"Of course I am. Who else?"

"Why should I hold anything against you?"

"Because I left you behind. Fled without you."

Amidst a downpour, Mathias and Nikki had fled the mansion by themselves. As a result Rita had arrested Bernhardt and put him in confinement. He had been forced to spend the last three months venturing out on the Night Harvest, alone and with his hands in chains.

Bernhardt brought those hands together over his stomach and leaned back in his chair. "Have you been feeling tormented? Utterly ridiculous. How so naive!"

"But—"

"This I can say for sure. I would have done the same, had I been in your position."

"That's—"

"Neither here nor there? Not at all. It's exactly the same. You see, I'm very good at standing in other people's shoes. I understand your reasons, as I understand Nikki's."

Mathias recalled the trip from Fuerth to Quinta. Did a soul

capable of standing in other people's shoes take lives so casually? Bernhardt had done just that to the unfortunate soldiers in charge of them.

"Anyway, what brings you here, Mathias? I doubt you came all this way to have this discussion. Cut to the chase!"

"Right. You're right." There was no point in arguing the matter with someone who insisted that he didn't bear a grudge. Mathias asked him, "How much do you know about Quinta's current affairs?"

"Let's say I'm not without a clue."

"Weren't you being kept by yourself?" Gabriele questioned, surprised.

"I chat with the guards on watch duty. So, no, I'm not completely isolated from events."

"Then I can summarize." Mathias explained how Rita was in charge of the district, how she was trying to maintain independence from the royal government, how an extreme surveillance society had been instituted, how "the plaza Titan" served to eliminate rebellious elements, and so on. He then described the current status of the resistance movement.

"I see. I'm a little concerned to hear Jarratt hasn't returned."

"Yes, me too." Bernhardt's former henchman, a muscular old man, Jarratt had left three months earlier with the aim of conveying Quinta's situation to Fuerth, but had yet to return. "He's not the kind of person to leave his friends to die, I take it?"

"No, he isn't." Bernhardt got up and looked in turn at Mathias and Gabriele. "I see your situation. Now, what exactly is it you would like me to do?"

"I have a request." Mathias took a breath, exhaled, then swallowed. *Better to just come out with it.* "I want you to slay the plaza Titan."

"What for?" Bernhardt's expression was unchanged.

"The Titan is a symbol of control and terror. By removing it we can instill some courage in people. We can create the circumstances necessary for a massive uprising."

"Why not ask this insider you spoke of? She would be privy to the security layout. It shouldn't be too difficult to kill a five-meter-class in restraints."

"The real problem is the soldiers. They guard the plaza in large numbers, all of them with firearms. Amanda... She says she doesn't want to be shot at. She won't do it."

"I can't say I fail to understand the sentiment," Bernhardt said, chuckling mischievously. "So you want me to do it, despite it being so dangerous?"

"Yes. There isn't anyone else."

"It's a lot to ask."

"I know. But for you, it wouldn't be impossible."

"Old man, you're tough, right? Why not give it a shot? This guy's tramped all this way in person just to see you," Gabriele goaded, then pointed his chin at the Vertical Maneuvering

Equipment. "That can get you back inside, yeah? Sounds like a good deal to me."

"True enough. But he said it himself, just a moment earlier." Glancing at Mathias, Bernhardt stretched his legs out and perched them on the edge of the well. "All in all, he's the one to blame for my current situation."

Hadn't he said just now that he'd have done the same in Mathias' position?

"Man…" Gabriele took yet another swig from the bottle. His eyes already showing signs of inebriation, he hiccupped and shoved it back. "You're pettier than you seem, assigning blame. This guy's pretty much begging for your help. Can't you oblige him? I mean, aren't you pissed off at those bastards yourself for how they've treated you?"

"Oh, *excuse* me."

Bernhardt held the bottle up and peered into the base. It was already empty. He tossed it into the well, and a splashing sound echoed from its depths. Apparently, it hadn't run dry yet.

"Your logic's a bit haphazard, but I like it. The gusto of it."

"Bloody cheek," Gabriele said, glowering.

Bernhardt broke into a grin, watching the younger man side-on. "Interesting. Mathias, you appear to have netted quite a character for this resistance of yours."

"So it seems."

Bernhardt was going to agree to do it. Mathias wasn't sure

how he knew, but he did. Maybe it was Gabriele's passionate outburst. If so, Mathias couldn't thank him enough.

"I accept."

Bernhardt swung his feet down from the well and got up. He tapped his fingers over the Vertical Maneuvering Equipment's rewinding apparatus, its anchors, and its levers.

"The plan is to fell the regime's symbol, the Titan, in plain sight of the masses. Most compelling." He winked theatrically in Gabriele's direction. "And your friend is right. I am angry, quite angry indeed. At all those bastards."

"That's more like it!" Gabriele got up too, but he was visibly swaying. He put a hand on the well for support and swiveled his chin towards the hut behind them. "Mind if I grab a few more?"

"We're going," Mathias told him.

The Harsh Mistress of the City

CHAPTER FIVE

In the middle of the night, Rita was at her desk in the executive chamber taking her first meal in close to ten hours. It consisted of hard bread, steamed potatoes, and a vegetable soup with just a few scraps of meat.

The food shortage was becoming severe. Even as the district's administrator—especially as its administrator—Rita couldn't allow herself to eat more extravagantly than the populace.

The young soldier by her side had volunteered to test her food for poison. He took a sip of her water, then sliced small portions off the surface and center of the bread and potatoes, and tried these too.

Over the last few weeks there had been a number of attempts on Rita's life. She had come close to being cut down in the streets, and had been shot at. No one had tried poison yet, but caution was her greatest ally. She couldn't afford to drop her guard, even here in the district hall.

The taster was the only person with her in the oversized chamber, but more guards were posted under the windows and in the corridor beyond the door.

Rita pulled in the mountain of reports her troops had brought her. Under the wavering candlelight, fully aware that it was bad manners, she scanned the reports as she ate.

Despite all of her devotion and hard work, the stream of residents who chose to act out of self-interest was endless. People who hid sheep that could be milked, who lied about their age to be excused from the Night Harvest—at least the majority had been arrested after their neighbors or family had turned them in.

Some of the reports were marked with black-red stains. Blood. The soldiers must have beaten the accused during the interrogation. It wasn't behavior that she actually welcomed, but no one admitted to crimes otherwise. She needed to give tacit approval to violence, as a necessary evil to get the swindlers and crooks to talk.

There was a knock at the door.

Her taster looked sharply up. Rita was more or less done with her meal. His job, she realized, had been completed a long time ago. Engrossed with the reports, it had slipped her mind to dismiss him.

"Come in," she said towards the door.

The face of one of her troops, still young, poked in through the gap. He was shortsighted and wearing glasses. Rita had come to value the boy lately. Despite his youth he was a fast thinker.

He entered the chamber and stood to attention, saluting.

"Reporting in! Eugen has admitted to plotting treason! He is also connected to the clandestine forces."

It took Rita a moment to process the words, but she remembered quickly enough.

Eugen. Among the soldiers who'd been left behind in Quinta, he was third in rank after Rita and Amanda. Rita had held him in fairly high regard, but recently she'd been tipped off that he might be connected to the rebels. She'd ordered a few of her subordinates to interrogate him.

"I see. That's unfortunate."

"Yes, indeed."

"And?"

"Pardon me?"

"Names, of traitors within the military. Did he give you any?"

"I...don't think so." His eyes moved nervously. Perhaps he was admonishing himself for having come in to report without obtaining all of the facts.

"Go and find out," Rita said, but immediately reconsidered it. "Actually, no. Have him brought to me."

"Yes. Right away."

The soldier saluted and bounded out of the room. Rita caught a fleeting glimpse of the troops standing guard in the corridor.

Her taster shifted uncomfortably by her side. He seemed unsure whether he should leave and whether he was even allowed to ask if he should.

"Stay a little more," Rita instructed. She wanted as many of her troops as possible to witness how she dealt with conspirators.

Soon afterwards, multiple footsteps approached. There was another knock at the door, and on Rita's acknowledgment it was flung open. Two soldiers came in, dragging another with them. He was built like a rock and had a craggy face to boot. The bespectacled soldier stood in wait behind them.

"Bring him here." Still seated, Rita flicked her eyes towards the space in front of her desk.

The bulky soldier, Eugen, was forced forwards, the two guards tugging him by the arms. His legs hung completely limp, and his toes scraped over the floor. Maybe they'd broken his kneecaps. His arms were also slack at either side. The tips of the fingers on his left hand were wrapped in layers of cloth, no doubt originally white but now stained and dark. They'd removed his fingernails. That was all it had taken—losing his fingernails on one hand and the use of his legs—for him to confess his crimes.

He was weaker than she'd thought.

The soldiers hurled him to the floor. One grabbed him by the hair, made him lie on his side, and yanked his head up. The other stood behind them keeping a watchful eye.

Rita nodded at the taster, who was still next to her. She glanced at the table, and he scrambled to put away the empty plates.

She examined Eugen anew. His once craggy face, severely beaten, was now swollen out of shape. His eyes were puffy and almost fully closed. Blood streaked his cheeks and jawline, swabbed unceremoniously away from his nose and broken lips.

"Is he conscious?"

Eugen's eyes opened a fraction, revealing that he was.

"Commander," he rasped. "Please…help."

"I will help you. Once you've told us everything you know."

"But I…haven't…"

"Didn't you admit it? Aren't you connected to the resistance?"

"I—"

"He did," interrupted the soldier still holding him by the hair.

The one behind them moved in and stamped down on the captive's toe.

A baritone cry issued from Eugen's mouth, a voice like an animal in its death throes. Tears trickled down from the slits that had been his eyes. His toenails must have been removed as well, and his shoes were probably filled with blood.

"Any other traitors? What info did you leak? How have you assisted them?"

"I… I…" Eugen repeated the self-same word.

The soldier standing behind him stamped down on his toe again—and again and again, putting all his weight on it each time.

Eugen writhed, screaming in agony and sending spittle into the air, then cowered into a slobbering ball. Shivers ran up and

down his frame.

"I betrayed you… I betrayed you!" he wailed, forcing his eyes open.

"What information have you leaked?"

"I…"

This time the soldier stepped on Eugen's knee and slowly started applying his weight.

Eugen spasmed violently. "P-Patrols, guard details!"

"Who was your contact?"

"Never…never the same person. Th-They come to me!"

"What else do you know about them?"

"What…I know…"

Eugen's pupils were darting around. His face was covered in an oily sweat.

It mixed with the dried blood already there.

Rita met the gaze of one of the soldiers.

Taking her meaning, he began to unsheathe the sword at his waist. There was the shrill sound of metal scraping against metal. Reflecting the candlelight, the blade cast fleeting sinews of light over the walls and the ceiling.

"M-Mathias! Mathias Kramer!" Eugen screeched.

Rita's hands squeezed into fists. She felt as though her blood had frozen and boiled over at the same time.

Mathias. Her friend, her childhood friend, who'd killed one of her boys. She'd discovered long ago that he led the resistance.

The intel was common knowledge amongst the Garrison.

It was nothing new. Yet to hear the name again, and in this fashion, shook Rita to her core.

He still expected her to be *his kind Rita.*

It was why she felt so let down.

"Commander!"

The urgency of the voice pulled Rita back to the chamber.

Eugen had somehow struggled to his feet. He shook off the soldiers' hold with an incredible display of brawn and charged at Rita, his hair disheveled, his eyes bloodshot.

He kicked the floor, soared over the desk, and extended his arm—

Crap, Rita bit her lip just as…Eugen halted in midair.

Then, as though time were running in reverse, he was jerked to his rear. His back collided into the floor. He rolled around groaning, and blood seeped out from a hole in his clothing near his buttocks.

Only just containing her amazement, Rita looked up.

Amanda was standing in the open doorway. She was in a crouch, her anchor-firing mechanism aimed in Rita's direction.

Rita immediately understood. Amanda had used the Vertical Maneuvering Equipment to fire an anchor into Eugen to winch him back. It must have been tugged loose and recovered just as soon.

"You okay?"

"Yeah, thanks," Rita expressed her gratitude.

Before her eyes the soldiers rushed to restrain Eugen and to bind him tightly with rope. She couldn't help thinking, *Why now?* He had neither the will nor the strength to mount any further resistance.

Amanda walked into the chamber. Glancing at Eugen and the soldiers in turn, she narrowed her eyes in disgust.

"Why the ruckus?"

"I was questioning him. This kid, he's with the resistance."

"Don't think you're overdoing it a little?"

"They don't tell the truth otherwise."

"I wonder." For a moment, Amanda regarded Eugen in silence. "Aren't you just making them say whatever it is you want to hear?"

"Amanda," the bespectacled soldier voiced a nervous protest.

She ignored him completely.

This is who she is. This is Amanda. She never thought twice about speaking her mind, regardless of whom she might be addressing. As a result, people tended to believe she wasn't two-faced.

"Maybe it's putting the screws like this," Amanda continued, "that's turning people against the military and giving rise to an organized resistance."

"I disagree," Rita countered without a pause. "If you aren't strict with them, people degenerate."

"Corner a fellow and he'll take extreme measures. What happened now is a perfect example."

Amanda pointed at Eugen. Bound many times over, he was sniveling and shedding tears from the pain.

Rita shook her head. "You're wrong. He wouldn't have told the truth if I'd been compassionate. He would have continued to leak inside info, degrading the whole situation in Quinta. I need to ensure that doesn't happen."

"I see." Amanda let out a small sigh. "Well, you're the king of these parts. I'll do what you tell me."

"Make sure you do. And…"

Rita surveyed the executive chamber. The soldiers who had brought Eugen in were hauling him to his feet. The bespectacled one was watching on with a tense look. The tester stood at her side, looking quite lost. Blood from Eugen's buttocks rudely stained the floor's wood panels.

Rita said to Amanda, "I owe you for your help just now, so I'll overlook it. But I advise you not to voice such opinions in the future."

"Guess I'll be going then," Amanda announced curtly, turning her back to Rita.

"Where to?"

"I've got patrols. Your decision?"

This jogged Rita's memory. A while ago, she had put Amanda in charge of late-night patrols. "Right. Take care."

"And you."

Amanda left, her footfalls silent.

"Acting commander," the bespectacled soldier said.

"Yes?"

"What should we do, regarding Eugen?"

"Continue his interrogation. If you don't mind, I'm going to take a little rest."

"Yes, please."

"You know what to do. Once you're done."

Rita heard the young soldier gulp. His eyes drifted in the direction of the plaza.

Suddenly interested, she asked, "Who tipped us off?"

"Oh, um…" the bespectacled solider hesitated.

"Yes?"

"The informant is from Eugen's year. They'd been in the same team since the beginning and were close, it seems. That's probably why he noticed."

"I see."

Rita had valued Eugen. She'd even granted him a large mansion for that reason. Perhaps his friend had become jealous. Perhaps that was why he'd jumped at the chance to inform on a teammate.

But no, she was wrong to look for malice. He'd fingered his friend out of a genuine wish to uphold order. Moved by Rita's principles.

"Eugen's mansion," she said, "will go to the soldier who turned him in. Tell him he is free to move in with his family."

"Yes, ma'am."

There was a sudden rush of footsteps, and another subordinate leapt into the room.

"What is it?"

"Intruders at the east wall! Please proceed to verify—"

"Intruders? What do you mean?"

"I don't have the details. But apparently fighting has broken out!"

"Understood. I'm leaving this place in your hands," Rita ordered the bespectacled soldier. Then she headed toward the door. "I can come now. Show me the way."

It would be another long night.

***

Gabriele had been shot.

His body tottered in the moonlight, tipping until, unbalanced, he fell from the fifty-meter wall.

"Gabriele!"

Mathias reflexively reached out with his left hand. The other was wrapped in cloth, fastened around the taut wire. His legs were balanced on the Vertical Maneuvering Equipment fixed around Bernhardt's waist.

The three of them had made their way back to the wall, scaled the exterior side, and begun to rappel down into Quinta itself. They had concealed themselves behind a cannon and gauged the interval between patrols. Having confirmed that the troops were far enough away, they'd finally commenced their descent. And yet…

They had been seen.

Mathias' hand fell short of Gabriele.

"Hold on!" Bernhardt said, immediately letting the wires out at full speed.

The two of them entered free-fall. Bernhardt landed a powerful kick on the surface of the wall. Their bodies curved away from the structure and floated into empty space.

Mathias' feet slipped from the Vertical Maneuvering Equipment. His hand came away from the wire. He, too, started to plummet towards the ground, forty meters below.

Snapping his left hand back in, he formed a ring with his arms and locked them around the wire. It bit into the inside of his elbows, all but tearing the fabric. He ended up suspended from that one point, and pain seared through him as his skin chafed.

Bernhardt stretched out his arms. He caught Gabriele's clothes in both hands and pulled him in. Then, somewhat awkwardly, he wrapped his legs around the man's small frame, securing him.

The wire flexed, and the three of them swung back towards the wall in the manner of a pendulum.

In the ring made by Mathias' arms, the wire danced madly. This time, it pressed against the upper part of his right arm. The one he'd broken.

He clenched his teeth against the pain but, unable to bear it, ended up screaming.

He had no time to prepare for the collision. Neither did Bernhardt.

They crashed into the wall.

Mathias seemed to have hit his shoulders, hips, and back. The impact momentarily banished all five of his senses, but the pain came almost immediately afterwards, excruciating, joined by the sensation of his innards rising to his throat.

He was left hanging behind Bernhardt's waist, his elbows hooked around the wire.

Above him Bernhardt's arms had formed a ring, too, around Gabriele's head, to lock him in place. The wounded man, still unconscious, was limp.

"Will he be okay?!"

"They got him in the shoulder. A mere flesh wound," Bernhardt made light of it.

Indeed, the area between Gabriele's left shoulder and elbow was stained dark red. He was still bleeding, and Mathias wanted to attend to the wound as soon as possible, but…

"It's that man!"

"He escaped! He's getting back in!"

"Get word to the captain!"

The group of soldiers shouting at one another above their heads had to be the ones who'd fired at Gabriele just a few moments earlier.

There was another volley of gunfire. The bullets grazed the air next to the hanging trio.

"Let's get to the other side of the road. Grab the belt and let go of the wire. It's going to get a little bumpy."

"Okay."

There was more gunfire. Two shots. Luckily, the bullets went farther astray.

The soldiers were likely unaccustomed to firing their guns. Granted, leaning out from a fifty-meter wall buffeted by strong winds and hitting a target that clung to the surface some ten meters down was no simple task. Perhaps it was an impossible one given the skill level of the rookies left to Quinta.

But it was too soon to relax.

A troop of them were looking up at them from the street directly below. It wouldn't be long before the shooting started from there too.

"Pardon me." Mathias hooked his legs around Bernhardt's waist, pulled himself slightly away, and took hold of the belt connected to the Vertical Maneuvering Equipment.

"Fine. Now then…"

His arms locked around Gabriele's body, Bernhardt brought his wrists as far to the left as they would go. He placed his fingers on one of the levers poking up from his waist.

The three bodies began to descend. As they did, Bernhardt adjusted the angle of the firing mechanism and shot a second wire diagonally downward. The anchor struck the roof of a three-storied building across the street next to the wall, audibly smashing into the tiles and jabbing deep into the surface. The Vertical Maneuvering Equipment had them suspended on two wires, one on either side.

"Time for a midair stroll."

Even with Gabriele in his grip, Bernhardt continued his expert manipulation of the Vertical Maneuvering Equipment. He seemed to be maintaining a uniform velocity for both wires as one was reeled in and the other was released. As a result, instead of falling, they were gliding at an angle through the air, towards the rooftop.

Caught in the moonlight, their shadows landed on the street below. The soldiers ran over these, shouting to each other, and Mathias could make out what they were saying before long.

"Will we make it?"

"Watch you don't bite your tongue!"

Heeding Bernhardt's advice, Mathias clamped his mouth shut. The roof was approaching. When they were just a couple of meters off, it suddenly felt like they were floating. They'd entered free-fall.

"Seems the wall-side wire popped—"

They crashed into the tiles before Bernhardt could finish.

Amidst another surge of agony, Mathias realized he'd let go of the Vertical Maneuvering Equipment's belt. He started to roll and hurtle across the tiles with frightening speed. His aching body reeled from impact after impact.

The roof slanted down towards the road. Realizing that he was on his way to falling headfirst from a three-storied building, Mathias unconsciously spread out his limbs. His left elbow, then his hand, struck the surface of the roof. He suffered another unbearable streak of pain as his fingers banged off and leapt up from a tile.

He kept sliding, now on his back. Yet he'd managed to kill some of his momentum, and the rolling had stopped.

Bit by bit he slowed before finally coming to a halt. Struggling to shut the pain out of his mind, he cautiously raised his head. He was right next to the edge.

That was close…

He rolled over to lie prone on the tiles. He raised his head a second time, still wary, and found Bernhardt crouched where the anchor had struck the roof and looking his way.

"Stay there."

Bernhardt let go of Gabriele and, unspooling the wire in

gradual increments, began to approach Mathias. His clothes, or rags, were stained dark with Gabriele's blood. He squatted down next to Mathias and glanced at his own waist.

"You should probably take hold."

"Thank you."

Mathias reached out and hooked his fingers on the Vertical Maneuvering Equipment's belt. As Bernhardt set the wire to wind back in towards his original position, Mathias let himself be pulled by the arms in a half-crouch.

Somehow making it to Gabriele's side, they surveyed their surroundings. Soldiers were running along the top of the wall, pointing down and shouting. There was a similar commotion coming from below. They had to get away, and as soon as possible.

"Can we use the rooftops?"

"At first, yes."

Bernhardt grabbed Gabriele by his clothes and hauled him up. Once again he formed a circle with his arms and fed Gabriele's head and shoulders through.

"Let me help."

"No need to be polite, I'm stronger." Bernhardt tugged his arms in, still cradling Gabriele, who was now bent at the waist. "They'll be up here soon. The smart thing to do would be to get to street level before that happens."

"Yes."

"That way."

Bernhardt motioned his jaw away from the wall. Then he set forth.

Mathias followed him from behind. It was difficult to keep his balance. His whole body was screaming, but he knew he had to put up with it.

"Time we headed down."

Bernhardt turned a right angle and stopped at the edge of the roof. Between them and the next building was an alley some three meters wide.

"I can't leap so far!"

"No need. Take hold of me."

In the same manner as they had at the wall, they lowered themselves to the ground. There were footsteps and male voices, rather close by. Soldiers were already running through the alleys in search of them.

"I suggest we split."

"And Gabriele? Will he be okay?"

"He'll be coming around anytime now."

Mathias doubted Bernhardt would say something like that just to set him at ease. If the man thought Gabriele was going to die, he would declare as much and coldly state that they were leaving the unlucky bastard behind.

It was true that the blood hadn't spread much.

"That's good to hear."

"Now where should we find each other?"

"There's a small bookstore, all the way into the bazaar. He knows the exact location," Mathias cast his eyes on the man in Bernhardt's arms.

"Wonderful. He shall be my guide."

"If you're having trouble you can ask someone. They'll know where if you ask for Derek's bookshop."

"Understood."

Bernhardt was a seasoned "outlaw" who seemed to have spent time in Quinta in the past. There was no need to worry. If there was anything to be concerned about, it was Mathias' own ability to escape.

"All right then…"

They swapped looks, then set off in separate directions.

They were near the edge of Quinta, but on the side that originally bordered the interior. The citizens living here had enjoyed comfort, and the houses were large. Most were empty now, though. The privileged had been the first to flee the district.

Mathias turned a corner each time he sensed someone nearby. He vaulted into whichever alley was narrower. At the same time he took care to move away from the wall and in towards Quinta's heart.

He was making his way down a winding street hemmed in on both sides by two-storied buildings when he came to a dead end.

This isn't my day…

There was a building in front of him, a commonplace brick structure with two floors. On his side there were no windows at street level, no foothold to scramble up on. Nor was there any tree, or even barrels or wooden boxes lying around.

He immediately made an about-face. There was an intersection just ten meters ahead.

A few figures appeared there.

The larger half of them had special-purpose blades slung in sheaths on their waists. The ones with rifles caught Mathias' attention, too. Even in the faint moonlight, the crests stitched to their chests were clearly the Garrison's.

He couldn't advance. But he doubted retreating would improve his fate.

"Shit," the crass word escaped his lips. That, too, he could never have imagined a year ago. Six months with outlaws had changed him in no small measure.

"Stay where you are!" came the interpellation.

What do I do? Should he surrender himself and wait for his comrades to break him free? Or should he try to fight his way through, hoping for the best?

Unable to decide, he almost stood still doing neither.

Just then, one of the soldiers punched one of the others in the pit of his stomach. When the unsuspecting victim doubled over, he had his head driven into the wall.

"Captain?!" a third soldier piped, the lantern in his hand illuminating his bewildered expression. This one suffered a gouging blow to the side of his head, crumpled onto his knees, and hit the ground. The soldier who'd kissed the wall lay limp next to him. The lantern, fallen too, flared all the more brightly for a second.

"What in the..."

Mathias stared at the soldier who had snapped—he assumed—pick up the hand lantern. The only one without a rifle, this "captain" instead wore the Vertical Maneuvering Equipment and twin sword sheaths. From below, the warm light illuminated her face.

Amanda was scowling hard.

"Must you be such a handful?"

"Right. 'Captain' meant you..."

"You're taking responsibility for this." She indicated the two soldiers sprawled by her feet. "This gets reported, I can't stay in the Garrison. I'll have to go into hiding."

Like Mathias, Klaus, and the others.

Is she going to kill them to protect her place in the Garrison? he suddenly feared, and asked as much. "You're not...silencing them, are you?"

"You can be a real ass, Mathias." She looked up again, and two cold eyes bore in on him. They conveyed her irritation. Of course she wouldn't silence them, which meant there was no going back for her thanks to him.

"I'm sorry." Relieved, Mathias dipped his head in apology.

"Maybe that isn't enough."

She looked away, then dropped into a crouch to pry a gun from one of the soldier's hands. She held it out. She was urging Mathias to take it.

He shook his head. He wouldn't use guns within the town limits. If possible, he didn't ever want to touch one again.

Amanda gave a loud snort but laid the gun down anyway. She knew Mathias' history. She wasn't going to insist.

"Follow me." She turned her back on the scene and started to run, lantern in hand.

"We managed to deliver the equipment. They found us when we came back over the wall."

"I know."

"Gabriele's still with him. I told him we'd meet at the bookstore."

"Got it."

Amanda appeared to know every backstreet in Quinta. She took lane after lane without a moment's hesitation. They passed the occasional pedestrian, residents who were night owls or who were up absurdly early, but never came across any soldiers.

They emerged into a broader street, one Mathias had never been on before.

Amanda came to a halt before a sturdy-looking but bland two-storied building made of stone. She stooped at the wooden door, put her lantern on the floor, and opened the lock. She'd been in possession of a matching key.

"Where are we? It doesn't look like a house…"

"This leads to the underground reservoir. We can use it to get through the net."

The net of soldiers blocking their way, Mathias supposed. "You're impressive," he said.

Without answering, Amanda picked up the hand lantern and stepped through the doorway.

The flickering flame illuminated a pitch-black corridor. They continued forwards until they came to another door. This one had no lock. They opened it to reveal a stone staircase leading a long way down.

The lantern's light cast their shadows against the wall. Mathias felt a stream of cold air on his skin. They had descended about two basement floors in a normal building.

The space opened up. There was a landing, and around it a black, glossy expanse of water. Countless stone pillars, spaced at regular intervals to support the high ceiling, rose from the surface like colossal trees.

"I didn't even know this place existed."

"That way."

Amanda raised the lantern, indicating something to the right. Alongside the wall there was a stone footpath about half a meter wide that appeared to wind around the entire area. It probably connected the landing they were on to others. Each would lead to another exit, and Quinta itself.

Mathias nodded and stepped onto the path. Amanda followed from behind, using the lantern to illuminate the way. The light reflected off the water, and whenever Mathias dislodged specks of sand, multiple ripples spread across the surface.

After a minute or so, he halted, sensing something.

"What is it?" Amanda asked from behind. She held the lantern out over the water, casting more light on the path ahead.

"There's something…"

Mathias realized what it was before he had finished.

Without any light source, and without making the faintest noise, someone was approaching them from the opposite direction.

She stopped just five meters away.

"Hello, Mathias."

It was Rita.

It was their first meeting in half a year.

Mathias had even avoided the public executions at the hands of the plaza Titan. Soldiers would be carrying flyers with his picture and looking for him.

Not for a single day in those six months had he not thought of Rita.

She looked as though she'd lost weight. Her cheeks were

sunken, her eyes severe. Her light blond hair was cropped short; that at least was unchanged. Gone, however, were all traces of her laid-back personality.

It was as though she was, in fact, another person entirely.

"Rita..."

What to say? There were so many things he wanted to tell her.

He'd imagined this moment, their meeting again, their having the chance to talk, over and over. What he would say first, what he would say second, Rita's reaction—he'd run a thousand different scenarios through his mind.

All of that was gone. He couldn't think of a single thing to say.

"Hello."

The one word, stupid, useless, was all he could muster.

Idiot, forget greetings. Apologize. Yes. First, apologize.

"Sorry."

He racked his brains for words to follow. But none came, however much he tried. He began to fret.

Rita watched him with an unreadable emotion in her eyes. Without a word, she drew the blade at her waist with an echoing screech of metal.

"Move out of the way."

The sound was matched from behind. Amanda's elongated shadow shifted angles. He realized she'd drawn her blade and

rested the lantern on the floor.

Mathias stayed where he was. He couldn't move.

"I want us to talk," he tried.

Rita said nothing in response. But nor did she cut him down.

"I…"

It was cold, and yet Mathias was covered in sweat.

"I wanted to help you. You had been left here, in Quinta. I thought I could help get you to the interior. For that, I needed to leave Fuerth and come—"

"I know," she cut him off. "That man told me."

"Then—"

"You said you came to help me?"

"I…"

"Were you trying to help me when you killed Duccio?"

The scene from half a year ago replayed itself in his head. The flash of the muzzle, the boy soldier's head exploding, all of it dissolving into a downpour.

"No… That was an accident. I hadn't meant to kill him."

His voice echoed amidst the pillars, the water, the walls, the ceiling. It was as though countless versions of himself were all speaking at once.

Rita opened her mouth, abruptly asking, "Am I so precious? For whom?"

Surprisingly, there was no sign of anger in her eyes. Nor sorrow. They were hollow, devoid of any message.

Mathias was unnerved, but responded, "You are. Of course you are..."

To me.

It hit him before he finished. He realized what Rita was trying to say.

Everything he thought he'd done to help her, to rescue her, he'd done for himself. It was to see her again, and nothing more, that he'd returned to Quinta.

If he *had* rescued her... That would have been nothing more, too. It wasn't for humanity's benefit that he'd tried to save her, to say the least.

Rita appeared to share the realization. She made a slight nod, her eyes still hollow. "I appreciate the sentiment. But it's misguided. It's wrong to consider your own happiness and nothing else."

Mathias had assumed the boy soldier's death had triggered Rita's rampage. That a desire for revenge had pushed her to initiate such extreme policing measures.

But the truth wasn't so clear-cut.

As the cause of Mathias' selfish behavior and the ensuing tragedy, perhaps she was feeling untoward guilt. Perhaps "eradicating all selfishness" had become her obsession for that reason.

Because Rita did not forgive selfishness.

She'd always been that way, in fact. She'd forsworn her own father, the man who'd left his daughter behind and killed himself in order to escape it all.

How had Mathias forgotten? It amazed him.

"You're right," he agreed. "I should never have come here. It was a mistake to even think about it. I should have stayed in Fuerth, prayed for your safety, and searched for something I could do from there. I accept that."

"If you believe it, disband the resistance. Turn yourselves in."

"We won't." Mathias shook his head. None of this altered what he needed to do. "I was wrong, but I don't think what you're doing now is exactly right, either. If I'm the one who started this, then I'm the one who ought to put an end to your rampage. To atone for my own actions."

"I'm not doing anything wrong." She drew her second blade and pointed it at him. "You see, I've decided to build a better world. I'll make this a place where nothing like that happens. And I'll do whatever I must."

"You're wrong to keep everyone imprisoned in such a dangerous place. You have to try to establish contact with the interior and begin evacuating."

"They abandoned us."

"That's not true. They just don't know the situation here."

"Why so sure?"

More than half a year had passed since Mathias' departure from Fuerth. He could hardly claim he knew how things stood in the interior.

"Either way," he insisted, "the district can't live on like this forever, completely isolated. There's a limit to how much food you can get from the Night Harvest."

"That's not all we're doing. We've started cultivating, and also, inside the wall—"

"How many people will it support, for how long?"

Mathias recalled what he'd been through only hours earlier. Attacked by a Titan, he'd sought refuge in a river only to be captured. He would have been eaten alive if not for Bernhardt.

"Forget cultivating anything outside the wall. I was just attacked by an aberrant Titan, not far from town. Does your 'better world' force people into facing that kind of danger?"

"Sorry, I'm getting bored."

The voice came not from ahead, but from behind Mathias.

It was accompanied by the hiss of compressed gas. Something raced past his right side, below his armpit, and straight towards Rita.

She swung her blade. A high clang, followed by a low thud. A blackish object struck the wall and fell onto the narrow path. It was an anchor from the Vertical Maneuvering Equipment. The wire led back past Mathias.

Amanda.

"Run," she said.

"But—" Mathias tried to turn around, but his clothes were yanked at his left shoulder. He lost his balance and began to lurch towards the pool of water. "Wha…?"

It had been Amanda. The stone wall, Rita, Amanda—they were all receding even as the two women stood with weapons drawn. Amanda reeled in her anchor and fired her other one. She charged as if to chase after it.

That was the last thing Mathias saw.

He hit the reservoir back first. His heart froze.

It was cold, much colder than the midnight stream.

He was sinking. It was dark. He couldn't make anything out, not even which way was up and which down. It felt as though he was being swallowed alive by some black, amorphous monster.

At any other time, he would have panicked. But right now, his safety was the last thing on his mind. It hardly mattered whether he lived or died.

What mattered was Rita.

Her heart had grown as cold and hard as ice. Thawing it would be no simple matter. The chances of persuading her here were almost nonexistent.

But he couldn't let time take its course. Every day, numerous residents were being made to take part in the Night Harvest. They lived under strict surveillance terrified of informants.

No, he had no choice but to take definite action.

First he had to end Rita's dominion over Quinta.

By force.

Without his realizing it, Mathias had floated back to the

surface. His face emerged from the water.

Up ahead, Rita and Amanda were locked in combat.

The latter seemed more proficient with the Vertical Maneuvering Equipment. While she deployed her blade with one hand, she used her other to repeatedly launch and reel in her anchors. She was firing them whenever even a little space opened, taking advantage of her opponent's distraction to step in and strike with her blade.

Meanwhile, Rita seemed adept at swordplay, employing two blades with precision to deflect Amanda's attacks in the nick of time.

"There are four exits, leave using the farthest!" Amanda said, holding her blade before her face and parrying Rita's blow.

Four exits. Meaning there would be stairs leading aboveground at each of the underground reservoir's four corners. He just needed to make for one.

"Got it!"

He wouldn't be of any use, even if he did try to help. And he wasn't puerile enough to insist on fleeing together. Amanda might defeat Rita and manage to escape. On the contrary, she might fall into Rita's hands. In that case...he'd push Bernhardt into fulfilling his role sooner.

All he could do was pray neither of them sustained severe injuries.

Pressing her sword in against her opponent's, Rita abruptly

released the blade from its hilt. The freed blade sailed into the air while Amanda's scythed above Rita's head. By then Rita had already swung her hand down and fixed the hilt to a new blade. She brought it up in a sweeping arc.

Amanda jumped back to evade the blow. Then came the sound of an anchor firing.

Mathias had a bad feeling about it…

He plunged his arms through the water, propelling himself forwards and ducking his head below the surface. Anchor and wire whistled overhead. They pierced behind him, formed bubbles, and were reeled back in immediately.

Rita had aimed for him, not Amanda.

Mathias surfaced for air.

"I'll find you, even if you run," Rita warned, still facing forward.

Mathias didn't respond, this time diving as far as he could into the water. He began to swim toward the wall at the opposite side from where Rita and Amanda stood.

It was difficult. He didn't really know how to swim. But he kept going, stifling his desire to breathe. It was dark, after all. From above Rita wouldn't be able to tell where he was.

No sooner than he thought this, an anchor and wire sliced diagonally past him. She'd fired again. Could she guess his approximate position, then, even without seeing him?

He couldn't hold his breath any longer.

His fingers found something hard and slimy. It had to be one of the columns. Disregarding the unpleasant sensation, and thanking his good luck, Mathias traced his way to the far side and swam up to the surface.

Poking out his head, he took a gasping breath. The stone column acted as a shield so he didn't need to worry about a direct line of fire.

He could hear metal clashing against metal. The fight continued.

He didn't even try to look their way.

He took another big gulp of air then, for the second time, plunged deep. He repeated the process of swimming to a pillar and raising his head out of the water.

I'll find you, even if you run, Rita's words replayed themselves in his head.

You're wrong, Mathias argued against the voice. *I'm the one who'll find you.*

He cut through half of Quinta, keeping to the backstreets wherever possible. His hair and clothes were all but dry by the time he finally arrived at the bazaar.

The bookstore was locked, but one of his comrades let him in as soon as he'd knocked and given the password. When Mathias proceeded towards the back, he saw that most of the resistance leaders were there. The store's owner, Derek, must have called an emergency meeting as soon as he'd received word of Bernhardt's rescue. Mathias saw Jodi for the first time since she'd handed him the Vertical Maneuvering Equipment by the gate.

Bernhardt was there too, sitting in the center and drinking warm tea like he owned the place. His handcuffs hadn't been removed, but the chain linking his wrists had been severed. He'd bathed and changed into clean clothes; he seemed to be in high spirits.

Klaus was leaning against a bookshelf, behind him, with his arms folded over his chest. Nikki, though, was nowhere to be seen. She was probably still asleep somewhere. She hated to be woken up, Mathias remembered. If someone had tried, to alert her to Bernhardt's rescue, it was entirely possible that she'd gone straight back to sleep after muttering, "Nice…"

Mathias' comrades were keeping their distance from Bernhardt. Everyone, the ones who were there at least, knew of his history with the Military Police Brigade and as an outlaw. With introductions out of the way, they were probably unsure as to how to deal with him.

A young man shrieked, upstairs. The voice had to be Gabriele's. It was enough to tell Mathias that he had made it.

Unsteadily, using the bookshelves for support, he walked towards the gathering.

Bernhardt caught sight of him and lowered his mug.

"Excellent, glad to see you again."

"You too." Mathias glanced up at the ceiling. "How's he doing?"

"Like I said, barely a flesh wound. They're taking care of it right now."

They could hear his voice. *Ow, stop that, damn it!*

"It doesn't sound like he's dying, at any rate."

Bernhardt nodded. "He likes to exaggerate."

"Here you go," Derek said, placing a wooden box to use as a chair.

Mathias thanked him and sat down. He scanned the faces of the resistance leaders assembled before him.

Jodi hesitantly raised her hand and asked, "Sorry, but what happened to Amanda? We heard she was on the run with you, Mathias."

"It's likely Rita got her."

As Mathias recounted the events from the underground reservoir, he couldn't stop his voice from shaking. The resistance leaders listened with solemn faces. But none showed any extremes of amazement or shock. Comrades being captured was hardly a new experience for them.

Mathias bowed his head. "I'm sorry. I left someone behind again."

"You did fine! You're in charge of this organization, I do believe?" Bernhardt indicated their surroundings with one of his usual dramatic gestures. "You're making progress. Why, that was a sound snap decision! Quite beyond you just half a year ago."

Bernhardt no doubt thought he was paying Mathias a compliment, but it didn't help lighten his heart.

"Still, this is a difficult situation," Derek said, swapping a couple of misplaced books that had caught his eye. "Amanda was Rita's closest aide. And we know she shows no mercy to traitors."

"She might end up suffering the same fate as him," someone noted, looking at Bernhardt.

"Which is why," Jodi said next, "we should act as soon as we can. Now that we have…" She gave Bernhardt a nervous look as though the chained "plaza Titan" itself were in the room with them. "Mr. Bernhardt? Now that we have him on our side."

"You're right," another leading member said, scratching his head. "We won't be able to get her out with any of our normal tricks. They're sure to have tightened their watch now that he's escaped. No, the only thing we can do now is overthrow the regime. If we pull that off we can get the lass out too."

By "the lass" he meant, of course, Amanda.

Loud stomping footsteps approached from above. The door to the stairs opened and Gabriele burst in with a bandage over his shoulder.

"The hero returns!"

Nobody responded.

Gabriele pouted, disappointed as he cast his eyes around.

"Nothing? It's thanks to my valiant efforts that the old guy's here. I think that deserves a little applause, a few whistles, maybe a speech in thanks—something, right?"

"You did well," Mathias said in acknowledgment.

"Put some feeling into it!"

"Amanda's been captured," Jodi told him with a grave expression.

Even Gabriele's darkened at this. "Really?"

"Really," Jodi said.

"We were saying how it would be difficult to get her out via conventional methods. That it was time to do something big."

"It was suggested, no more," Derek corrected, studying Bernhardt out of the corner of his eye. "Personally, I'm inclined to agree. Our ranks have grown in the last few months. Killing the plaza Titan might be enough to set things in motion."

"Well, I don't like it." Klaus unfolded his arms. "We should be the ones deciding whether or not we kill the Titan."

Jodi's eyes stretched wide. "We rescued your friend."

"So? No one told me it was on condition of slaying the Titan."

Bernhardt nodded at this, looking mischievous. "Indeed. I don't remember ever making such a promise."

"What?!" Jodi half shrieked.

Mathias knew not to be concerned. Bernhardt was eccentric to the point of pronouncing the idea of killing the plaza Titan as "compelling," and Klaus was simply against the idea of people taking their assistance for granted.

Bernhardt swept his gaze around the room. He took his time, savoring the focus, the looks filled with anxiety, suspense, hope. Then he breathed out and smiled broadly.

"Not that I see any reason to say no. We could go right now, if you'd prefer?"

The comrades all breathed a sigh of relief.

"We appreciate it," Mathias said, thanking Bernhardt again.

"It's my pleasure. As I believe I told you outside the wall, I'm angry at them too. I'm a man who values respect more than anything else. They lack it."

"Yes, I understand."

"All right, then." Derek got to his feet. "Mr. Bernhardt will help us slay the plaza Titan. Once this is done, we call upon Quinta's population to rise up. Are we in agreement?"

Jodi's chest was flushed red with excitement. "The sooner we do this the better."

The others had fire in their eyes as well. No one showed any signs of opposing the plan.

Klaus was still moody with his arms folded, but Mathias suspected he would cooperate when the time came.

"Hey, you guys. I think someone's here?" Gabriele held a finger to his mouth.

They all fell silent.

Someone was certainly knocking at the door. One knock,

followed by a pause and three more knocks, another pause, and one final knock. It was the code of the resistance.

"I'll go." Always helpful, Jodi was the first on her feet.

She hurried through the bookshelves. They heard the door opening, and when Jodi returned, it was with Nikki in tow. Mathias was on the verge of taking her through the plan, but when he saw the expression on her face, he stopped himself. There was nothing of her usual easygoing manner.

"I just heard, on my way here." Casting her eyes on the books piled up on the floor, Nikki drooped her shoulders. "They've scheduled a special public execution for this afternoon. They're going to feed Amanda to the Titan."

Five in the afternoon.

Mathias and the others stood hiding amidst the crowd under the powerful rays of the late afternoon sun.

After Nikki had delivered her news some ten hours earlier, Bernhardt had spoken up: "Perfect! This is exactly what we needed. We can butcher their authority if we're able to kill the Titan during a public execution. There'll be no more reason to fear the soldiers. And if I'm doing this anyway, I hope to do it in front of a crowd. It'll be much more effective!"

Mathias saw his point, but it felt excessive to carry out their plan in the middle of a public execution. With so many people gathered there in one place…

"People will get hurt."

"Your plan is to stage an uprising, yes? You can't overthrow a regime without spilling a little blood. You'd do well to stop pretending otherwise."

"We don't have enough time to prepare!"

"It'll work out if everyone pitches in. You have people throughout Quinta, I hear. It seems the movement has been growing rapidly. You have a hundred now? Two hundred? In any case, it's better to work on a tight schedule."

"But it has to be a trap. She's baiting us!"

"That's fine. We just need to make sure we don't fall into it."

The plaza was already packed full. It was suffocating just to stand there hemmed in on all sides. Vying to get a better view, people were leaning forwards, stretching up, squinting their eyes. There was little conversation but they were clearly fired up. Not for the first time, Mathias felt that things were abnormal. Quinta's residents lived in fear of being informed on, of being arrested, yet attended public executions with great fervor.

Perhaps it was the need to feel reassured that they, at least, were still safe.

Only the semicircular space before the district hall remained, as always, empty of people. The Titan sat crossed-legged in the center. It wore its usual melancholic look. Even on its haunches, it was two floors tall.

Heavy chains circling its neck, torso, arms, and legs spread out in a radial pattern and connected to mechanisms like the one used to open and close a gate. Each of these was fixed securely to the ground by a number of stakes. There had to be twenty or thirty of the mechanisms. Some had soldiers standing at either side, others didn't.

Wooden scaffolding, set up in front of the Titan, reached the district hall's third-floor balcony, the notorious gallows.

Rita, along with her soldiers, had yet to appear. The windows were shrouded by curtains.

They would show themselves soon enough.

With Amanda in tow.

Ready to sentence her to death.

The soldiers had made a special effort to publicize the special execution. No doubt they meant to entice Mathias and the members of the resistance, but even if none of them showed up, such a salient instance of a rebel's fate was bound to strengthen the regime's hold over the masses.

In other words, the plan couldn't fail.

"I must say I'm feeling the nerves!"

Bernhardt lifted his hands above the crowd and rolled his wrists. His handcuffs were gone. Craftsmen sympathetic to the cause had exercised their expertise. Still, and although his hair had been cropped short and his beard shaved as a disguise, anyone who knew his face might recognize Bernhardt.

"Well, it doesn't show."

If there was anyone still relaxed among them, it was Bernhardt. Concealed beneath his overcoat were the Vertical Maneuvering Equipment and the specialized blades.

They were some twenty meters from the edge of the crowd. Mathias would have preferred to get closer to the Titan, but that would risk revealing themselves to the Garrison.

"Remember what to do?" he asked Bernhardt.

"Remember who you're talking to?"

"Gotta say, you don't lack confidence, old man."

Gabriele had been keeping careful watch. He was to Mathias' right, while Bernhardt stood behind the two of them.

The plan was to move into action the moment Rita came into view. First, Mathias and Gabriele would clear a path, forcing people out of the way. Bernhardt would then leap or climb over Mathias and fire an anchor towards the Titan. From there he would sail through the air to assault the creature. Simultaneously, members of the resistance seeded throughout the plaza would pounce on the guards. Others, positioned in the crowd, would fire their rifles at the gun-wielding troops atop the buildings. This would prevent Bernhardt from being shot to pieces along with the Titan.

If Bernhardt managed to slay the Titan, it was Mathias' turn to act. He would proceed to the front of the plaza and call upon the residents to rise up. He was nervous about addressing a crowd, but it wasn't a role he could delegate.

Rita, of course, would do whatever she could to obstruct them. They had to make sure she couldn't act. For this, they had to rely on rifles. She might get injured in the process; depending on the case, she might even lose her life. Mathias found the idea more distressing than the thought of being injured himself, but they needed to go through with this.

Rita was after him with the same determination.

"Hey, old man, you'll have to show me how to use this someday." Gabriele gave a couple of hearty slaps on Bernhardt's back, that is to say, on the Vertical Maneuvering Equipment under his overcoat.

"I don't see why not. Although I must insist you stop calling me that."

"You are getting on though, old man."

"The appellation lacks any hint of glory."

"Maybe you're not as glorious as you think."

"Ah, the gall. Well, I will at least *consider* teaching you the use of this thing."

"She still hasn't shown," Mathias said, gazing up at the district hall.

The execution had been due to start some while ago, but the window curtains hadn't so much as fluttered.

Mathias felt a momentary urge to call the plan into motion anyway but thought better of it. They had to kill the Titan in front of Rita. To enable the residents to overcome their fear of her. To show her the true extent of their anger and sorrow. And yet the key element, Rita herself, was failing to materialize.

As the sun started to lose its erstwhile glare, the crowd began to grow restless.

"I wonder if something happened…"

"Like what?" Gabriele scowled, brusquely wiping sweat from his forehead.

"Maybe the plan got out."

"Everything's fine. You know, you worry too much."

"Maybe."

The moment he'd said this, Mathias heard a series of agitated voices from behind.

"Hey!"

"What the…"

Mathias turned without thinking to see Bernhardt shaking on tiptoes with his eyes rolled up, his chest puffed out, and his arms stretched down unnaturally straight.

The residents around him seemed creeped out and were shrinking away, trying to get some distance.

"Bernhardt?" Mathias made to reach out, but drew his hand back.

The man was convulsing violently, his torso arched like a bow. His face spasmed as though in laughter. He didn't respond to Mathias; his mouth was open, but the only sound to emerge was a retching from deep inside his throat.

His forehead was suffused with an oily sweat that reflected the sun's waning rays.

Arching even further, the pose hardly human, Bernhardt's body teetered backwards.

"Bernhardt!"

Mathias stepped in to catch the toppling form but came up short. Nearly supine, with nary an attempt to cushion the fall, the supposedly resilient outlaw was sinking to the ground.

The back of his head hit the cobblestone with a dull, disconcerting noise. Even then the convulsions continued, and his body lurched onto its side. Blood flowed from the back of his head, and dribble from his mouth.

People were screaming and jumping away.

"Bernhardt, are you okay? What's going on?!"

Mathias fell into a crouch. He grabbed Bernhardt by the shoulder and tried to get him onto his back, but the fierce convulsions kept knocking his fingers away.

Froth bubbled from the man's mouth, and he let out a keening cry that sounded more animal than human.

"About bloody time," Gabriele's nonplussed voice sounded from above.

Mathias craned his neck to look up at him. "Call for help! Do something!"

"I don't think so," the young man said. From near his chest he pulled out a thumb-sized vial. It seemed to have been hanging from his neck on a leather cord.

"Gabriele?"

"Probably should've used the whole thing." He held the vial up to the sun. It was still half full. "Nah, he'd have noticed."

What is that? Why isn't he shocked by Bernhardt's transformation?

"Ah yes, first things first." Crouching down next to Mathias, Gabriele took hold of Bernhardt's overcoat and pulled it open. The concealed Vertical Maneuvering Equipment came into view along with the twin blades. "I should probably requisition this—always pays to be careful." He'd pulled out a dagger from somewhere. Making deft use of it he set about cutting the leather straps that secured the equipment. It came free and clunked on the cobblestone.

Bernhardt's convulsions were already weakening and feeble. His heart-wrenching cries had subsided, too.

"What on earth," Mathias barely managed to ask.

Even as he spoke, a number of burly men pushed through the crowd. They approached until they were behind him and reached around from both sides. They grabbed and twisted his wrists and started dragging him away from Bernhardt. The pain was enough to make him whimper.

He was stumped. He realized he should resist, but he was too dazed even to command his limbs.

"Doesn't it speak for itself?"

He turned towards Gabriele's voice.

Mathias simply couldn't process what was happening to him.

"What do you mean?"

He saw it after he said this. Similar events were happening not just around him but across the whole plaza. He could hear screaming and swearing. Fights were breaking out. At the center of each disturbance, one or two men or women were being set upon and detained by a greater number of men and women.

"They're all…resistance?"

"Uh huh. A mass arrest."

"Why?"

"Because I reported what they looked like and where they'd be. Why else?"

The men on either side of Mathias forced him to turn around.

Out of the corner of his eye he could see Bernhardt being dragged by his overcoat by two oversized men. He was still arched backwards, but his convulsions had finally stopped. A grotesque smile was pinned to his hollowed-out features. A gap in the overcoat gave Mathias a glimpse of Bernhardt's groin. It was discolored, black and damp. He had, it seemed, lost control of his bladder.

For whatever reason, that was when Mathias finally understood that the man was dead.

Dragging his corpse and shouting "Make way! Garrison

coming through," the hulking men boisterously waded through the crowd.

Mathias, his hands still in a lock, was also being hauled away. His face ran into people's backs and shoulders. He didn't feel any pain, though. He was too bewildered for that.

Gabriele followed from behind.

Cutting a path through the confused crowd, they approached the chained Titan. When they emerged from the throng, they were in an open area in front of the district hall. The soldiers manning the winding mechanisms around the Titan cast nervous looks at Mathias and Bernhardt.

Mathias, who was still being forced along by the men, turned just his neck.

"You betrayed us. You chose Rita, over us."

"Not exactly." Gabriele laced his hands together behind his head. "I was never on your side to begin with. Had you from the start. So, not a betrayal."

"You were serving Rita from the outset, then."

"Wrong again. Sorry it's a little complicated."

Gabriele lifted his eyes, and Mathias stretched his neck to follow his gaze.

Troops were now lined up on the wooden platform—with Rita in the middle. Amanda was there too, farther back and restrained by soldiers.

When had they appeared? Rita was looking down at Mathias,

the expression in her eyes inscrutable. Without a doubt, she was aware of everything happening in the plaza.

Mathias was made to walk towards the scaffolding right past the Titan. The monster seemed almost close enough to touch, and he registered its peculiar heat. He could hear it breathing. Once they reached the foot of the wooden structure, he could no longer see Rita.

"You're a decent guy. I'll make an exception and tell you," Gabriele said from behind.

The soldiers yanked Mathias by the arms, and he continued forwards. They proceeded along the scaffolding and through the entrance, between the soldiers standing guard, to enter the cool, dimly lit district hall. The clamor of the crowd was suddenly far away.

"I was lying when I said I came from a small village. And about spending the last six months alone and on the run in the exterior."

It didn't make any sense. Gabriele had known where to wait during the daytime to evade the Titans. Together they'd spent a whole day in a narrow gap in a cliff.

"The bit about losing my horse was true, mind. But I didn't find it outside, I'd had it from the start. I got you good, didn't I?"

They took Mathias to the staircase. He noticed there were fewer soldiers around him now. Bernhardt had been carried off somewhere.

Gabriele continued to talk as they climbed the stairs. "I may not look it, but I'm a Fuerth official. Young for it, I know, but I do get by thanks to my folks' connections. You're from a rich family too, right? Bookstore guy told me. I expect you know all about that sort of thing."

Could he really be an official? Attached to the royal government? If so, what on earth was he doing here in Quinta?

"I'll give it to you from the top. Three months ago, one of your friends shows up at our place."

Indeed, the resistance had sent Jarratt to Fuerth. He was supposed to communicate what was happening in Quinta in order to request immediate assistance.

"We're at a complete loss. See, we just assumed everyone in Quinta was dead. We aren't in any position to respond to a call for help. We're lacking food ourselves."

"And Jarratt?"

"Hmm?"

"The elderly gentleman we sent. Well-built."

"Oh, that old fogey?" It sounded as though Gabriele might have received Jarratt's report in person. "I don't know. Maybe he's in jail, maybe they killed him."

"Why?"

"We've got a whole load of evacuees from Quinta. It wouldn't do for anyone to go around spreading unnecessary talk. Like I said, we're short on food ourselves. I mean, we're okay for now, but we definitely don't have enough going forward. If everyone was like, 'Let's help the people in Quinta, let's bring them here,' it'd be a fiasco."

"And so..." *they killed Jarratt?*

Incredible.

The stairs ended, and they reached the third floor. Mathias was pushed down the hallway to be stood outside a large wooden door.

"Anyway, back to my story." Gabriele nodded at one of the guards then turned back to face Mathias. "We decide that someone needs to come and check on the situation here, see if this old fogey's stories are true. It falls on me, as I'm one of their best. Smart, athletic, good at making snap decisions."

The guard knocked and announced their arrival. The door immediately swung into the corridor.

"So I leave Fuerth and am almost here...when my horse gets hurt and collapses on me. Like I said, even I start to fret at that point. I get here anyway, though. I'm good like that. I spend the day inside our cliff and make my way over to the orchard."

"Where you found Klaus' group at night."

"Yup."

The guard moved to one side. The two soldiers who had pretended to be civilians guided him into the chamber.

There were shelves filled with papers, a writing desk, some chairs and a table for receiving guests. The room was similar to

Mathias' father Jörg's study.

They crossed it and stepped through the windows.

Mathias squinted at the brightness. The wind was stronger than it had been below. The balcony before them led to the top of the wooden scaffolding. At its center Rita turned around to study Mathias through the line of soldiers.

Amanda's hands appeared to be tied behind her back. Although her face was blocked from view by her guards, Mathias could readily picture her sour look.

"I told him the story," Gabriele called out to Rita over Mathias' shoulder. "Didn't think you'd mind?"

"Nope."

Pushed in the back, Mathias advanced. People gazed at him from below.

The commotion had apparently settled. All around the plaza, resistance members had been detained and pulled away from the crowd.

Rita indicated Gabriele with a glance. "We've known each other for a couple of weeks. He told me everything, how he'd entered from outside and fallen in with your lot."

"Our interests coincided, as they say. Fuerth doesn't want refugees. Yet you and the resistance want to leave Quinta. This young lady, on the other hand, is of the opinion that all residents should stay here."

And so he informed on the resistance?

"I refrained from taking immediate action," Rita divulged. "Instead, I asked Gabriele to keep it up. I had him find out the names of your leaders, the location of your hideout, your next move."

"You know I had a great time?"

"If it was just arresting the leaders, I could do it anytime. But that alone wouldn't have meant much. I needed to round up every last member to demonstrate to the people of Quinta that it doesn't pay to be involved in wrongdoing."

Wrongdoing—the word choice bothered Mathias, but that was a trifle. "So you knew the whole time. That we planned to rescue Bernhardt and to stage an uprising."

"Of course. That's why I arrested Amanda." She glanced at her former colleague standing beside her. "With such material, I knew you'd play into my hands."

The platform, not entirely stable, swayed a bit each time the wind picked up. Moreover, unlike the balcony, it had no fence or guardrail. Leaning too far over the edge meant tumbling head-first into the cobblestones below.

Gabriele spoke again. "As for that older guy being kinda tough, the young lady here came up with an easy solution."

That was when Mathias finally caught up. "You poisoned him..."

Henning, Rita's father—adoptive father, to be precise—had seen fit to brew a lethal mixture for residents who wished to take their own lives. It was because this had come to light that he'd been fed to the Titan in that very plaza.

Rita must have kept some of the poison. Gabriele had received it from her and mixed it into Bernhardt's meal.

"How could you…" Bernhardt had died a dog's death. Literally, dispatched with poisoned food. "Why?"

Mathias tried to accost Rita, but the guards stopped him before he'd moved one meter. Pain sparked from his shoulder through to the top of his head as they twisted his arm even tighter.

He asked Rita regardless: "Why cooperate with them?"

"What do you mean?"

"Fuerth wants to abandon us. Their only goal is to save themselves. Isn't that exactly the kind of unforgivable behavior you hate?"

"I'm not forgiving it. But it's not a problem we can solve by turning up on their doorstep. That would only cost us more lives. I have to put the people of Quinta ahead of my own feelings."

"And so we reached an agreement," Gabriele said. "Quinta will be free of royal government interference, a city unto itself. Pretending not to have seen a thing, I return to Fuerth. That's the promise we made."

"But that's…"

Rita was in thrall to the idea of building a utopia where she was. Perhaps she couldn't maintain her equilibrium any other way.

"That's impossible, however you think of it. As I said this morning, we can't subsist within these walls!"

"We'll use the exterior, too."

"Things will become unbearable."

"The exact opposite. They'll get used to it, soon enough. I'll make them get used to it."

"What kind of world—"

"Admit it."

Rita glanced at the guards, giving them the signal. They took hold of Mathias' wrists and pushed him forward by his shoulders. The soldiers next to Rita moved out of the way. Mathias was shoved through the opening, to the edge of the platform.

The view opened up before him.

The people of Quinta stood in a ring, a huge big ring. The Titan sat enshrined at the center, below Mathias and slightly off to the side.

It slowly faced up. The chains around its neck emitted a shrill groan.

It looked so melancholic.

"I was right, help is not on the way. No one will aid us."

"Even then…"

Mathias tried to meet her eyes, but the guards prevented him from doing so. All he could do was face the Titan. Less than three meters separated them.

Nodding at the soldier next to her, Rita said, "Bye."

Footsteps sounded behind Mathias as one of the soldiers came to stand next to him.

Raising a pale sheet of parchment, he began, "This man, Mathias Kramer…"

The charges against Mathias were read out loud: Breaking and entering with larcenous intent. Murdering a soldier. Partaking in the Night Harvest under a false identity. Disallowing the original participant from fulfilling his duty. Aiding a criminal's escape. Trespassing on a forbidden area. Assembling with intent to disturb the peace. Amassing weapons…

There were too many to count.

Eyes as large as a baby's head examined Mathias; to its right and to its left, the plaza Titan had its palms flat against the ground. Its haunches seemed to have risen up a fraction.

It was possible it knew it was going to be fed.

The soldier continued, the list seemingly endless.

The crowd observed. None of them could save Mathias.

He was going to die.

Rita was going to kill him.

He felt a sting of regret. He wanted, there at the end, to be hearing her voice—not the young soldier's strained tones, but her soft ones.

Then he noticed it.

For some reason the residents were looking away, one after

another. Away to Mathias' left, southward.

Maybe they were getting bored. *Hurry up and throw him off, feed him to the Titan!* If that was what they were signaling, though, why were they all looking in the same direction? It wasn't part of the ritual as far as Mathias knew; even he'd have heard of such a thing.

The crowd began to stir.

At first the change was limited to a small part, but it began to spread, like a wave, until virtually all of them had their attention focused southward. Some were pointing up at the sky, interjecting with frozen expressions…

Mathias, too, craned his neck.

Turning to face south as well, the soldiers on the platform had their faces angled up.

In the distance, atop the wall surrounding the district, was a small black lump.

It grew larger until a face, then bare shoulders and a chest, became visible. Walking along the top of the great wall that stretched far to the south was a stark-naked man.

Had a pervert clambered up there without the soldiers realizing? Or had one of the soldiers themselves lost it and stripped bare?

No, that wasn't it.

"Titan…" the word escaped Mathias' lips.

Impossible.

A Titan on the small side was approaching Quinta on Wall Maria itself.

Screams exploded throughout the plaza.

The crowd began to stampede to the avenue on the north. Jostled, their clothes pulled, tripping, one after another they fell, to be trampled on by others coming up from behind. The crowd clambered over itself, angry shouts mixing with the screaming.

It was lucky there were no children—no parent wanted their own to see a feeding Titan—but the elderly and weaker women were being thrown aside, knocked down, kicked, and left behind.

Just as Mathias thought it was the only Titan approaching, a second came into view. As they were on a fifty-meter wall, they seemed small, but had to be at least three meters tall. This was clear in comparison to the cannons lined along the way.

Catching its foot on a set of rails there to move the weapons, the first Titan flapped its arms.

"Swords. And the Vertical Maneuvering Equipment," Amanda's cold voice rang out.

Everyone on the platform turned to look at her. They were all frozen to the spot, unable to process what was happening. Rita was no different, the color drained from her face, her hands half open and trembling.

"Forget executions and who's a rebel. Anyone who can use the Vertical Maneuvering Equipment, head out. Everyone else

needs to handle the crowd."

"They've come crossing," one of the soldiers groaned, his gaze fixed on the wall. "They must have climbed up in Shiganshina, then walked all this way..."

Getting up and down the wall was mostly done via a system of ropes, pulleys, and gondola lifts. But perhaps some districts featured staircases, and that was how the Titans had found their way up. Not that they'd actually decided to "use the wall to cross into another district"—they weren't intelligent creatures. They must have wandered up by chance sometime during the last six months and just carried on walking in search of people, until they happened upon Quinta.

"Who cares how," Amanda snapped. "Rita. Give the order."

"Oh. Right..." The acting commander seemed unable to pull her gaze from the south wall.

The first Titan turned west, onto the circular wall that ran around Quinta. The path ahead of it was dotted with cannons, next to which stood small figures.

Soldiers.

"Bad news..."

By now even Gabriele's voice was shaking. The troops on top of the wall seemed paralyzed, unable to take a step despite the Titan coming their way.

One of its arms reached out.

Long fingers clamped around the head of one of the soldiers

and squeezed, instantly pulping it.

The others, caught in the shower of blood, came back to life only to scream and run, in no state to fight back. One disoriented soldier fled in the wrong direction and lost his footing at the edge of the wall. He plummeted towards the ground, letting go of his rifle, his arms whirling in the air. He wasn't wearing the Vertical Maneuvering Equipment. Nothing could save him from the fall.

Mathias was about to avert his eyes but quickly pulled them back. He swallowed.

The screams in the plaza became even louder.

Another Titan came into view atop the wall. Considerably bigger than the first two, it had to be a seven-meter-class.

The wall was five meters wide at the top. Any Titan under ten meters could traverse it without difficulty.

The seven-meter-class paused near the edge. It looked out at the town sprawling beneath it. Its expression was too distant to make out.

Incredibly, it sauntered off the edge. Still upright, its hair swept back and its arms spread wide, it hurtled down. This was a fifty-meter drop. It couldn't possibly emerge unscathed.

Sure enough, a boom like cannon fire sounded, sundering a roof and throwing up a nimbus cloud of steam and dust at the point of impact. The vapor was the kind a Titan shed from its wounds. In other words, it had taken severe damage in the fall.

Its bones broken, skewering through skin. Its flesh ripped,

squashed, splattered…

That was when Mathias remembered.

A Titan didn't die unless the nape of its neck was sliced out.

No doubt the creature was quickly regenerating right there amidst the steam and dust.

"So many?" someone rasped.

The cloud had distracted Mathias, but he now saw even more of them atop the wall: a scrawny Titan, an abnormally potbellied Titan, a bowlegged Titan, a hunchbacked Titan… They ranged from three to seven meters.

All were approaching with meandering steps.

Then, tipping forward, a Titan with bedraggled hair that came to its chest fell headfirst off the wall.

"Holy…"

Staggering, Gabriele held onto a nearby soldier by the shoulder.

Another Titan rolled sideways off the wall, another huddling its knees, another extending its arms like wings. Each with its chosen pose, they hurled themselves from the wall without the slightest reluctance as though nothing was more natural.

It looked like a mass suicide.

Thunderous peals continued to ring out, and the endless clouds of steam and dust blanketed the town. The southern limits of Quinta were turning a uniform white.

"Rita!"

Rita's body shook at Amanda's razor-edged cry.

A haphazard evacuation was still underway in the plaza below. Many of the residents were in a state of panic. Amongst them, pulled down by the chains each time it tried to stand, the plaza Titan swiveled its head, taking in the scrambling masses with a most melancholic expression.

Rita took a deep breath. She closed her eyes for one second—no longer—then opened them again.

"Fetch Amanda's equipment and weapons! Gather all civilians before the east gate. Prepare horses, and food!"

"You're giving up on Quinta?" asked one of the soldiers, stunned.

Rita averted her eyes. "Yes. If those were all, we may have had a chance of winning."

"Ten or a hundred times as many could be on their way. There's no guarantee that isn't the case," Amanda said, turning to hold out her bound wrists to the soldier as though ordering him to remove them immediately.

The soldier hurried to comply.

Frowning a little, Amanda said, "It isn't safe here, not anymore."

"It'll be dangerous." Rita's hand was clasped tight over a hilt. Her knuckles were white. "But we're all leaving for Fuerth, on foot."

"Wait," Gabriele cut in, "what do you think you're saying? I told you, we don't want you!"

"The situation's changed." Rita pulled out one of her blades. "Fuerth will take us. I won't let anyone get in the way."

"Have you gone mad? It's still afternoon! There are Titans out there, too. You'll get attacked, all right?! Even if you did wait for nightfall, you can't travel to Fuerth in half a day!"

"Maybe. But we have to try, even if it means getting wiped out… Wouldn't that suit you? The royal government, I mean. You want us all to die."

"Don't make me spell it out. And…God forbid, you might actually make it…"

"We'll deal with that when it happens."

Mathias wanted to swallow but couldn't. His mouth had dried up completely.

Rita had decided to abandon everything she'd spent the last half-year building. In that scant second she'd had her eyes closed.

How did she do it?

How could she be so strong?

It had to be enough to tear her apart. He wouldn't have been surprised if her mind had simply ground to a halt.

No, maybe it had.

Maybe she was acting mechanically, like a cog, simply obeying her principle of protecting the residents.

"Let…"

Mathias had opened his mouth and taken a step before he

realized. By now none of the soldiers tried to stop him, and he was allowed to walk freely.

"Let me help."

He looked out over the plaza. People, out of their minds, were tumbling over one another, struggling to get as far away from the Titans as they could.

There was a young woman striking an elderly woman by the narrow exit; a middle-aged woman yanking a middle-aged man out of the way; a woman cradling an infant and trampling over a fallen, screaming youth. The doors of houses lining the street had flung open, ejecting people burdened with luggage who were sucked into the desperate stampede. They flew into a rage when their things were pulled away and launched themselves at anyone in their path.

A thin layer of vapor drifted through the air above them, sparkling in the light of the dipping sun.

"I can help with the wounded. At least let me do that."

I'm powerless.

It was the truth, and it made him want to cry.

"And set my comrades free. They'll be willing to help."

He believed it, too. The members of the resistance—more than anyone—would be willing to sacrifice themselves if it meant delivering the people of Quinta to safety.

"All right. Got it."

"We're running out of time," Amanda said, glaring up at the

wall.

She had already been given her Vertical Maneuvering Equipment and was almost done putting it on.

Rita tucked in her chin in the way of a nod and walked to the edge of the platform. Once there she fired an anchor and leapt into the air. The wire immediately whisked her away toward the southern avenue.

Amanda followed along with the other soldiers.

None had wasted a single word on sentiment.

They landed on surfaces lining their path, crouching to cushion the impact and firing their next anchors in almost the same moment. They soared over the fleeing crowd in the opposite direction, with a trajectory like lightning, closing in on the danger.

It had happened all so quickly, in the blink of an eye.

Mathias rubbed his arms. They felt wrong from being held in place for so long. Gabriele was there next to him, cursing and stamping his feet. They were the only two left on the platform.

Mathias pushed the fellow out of the way and began to make his way downstairs.

***

Rita kept fighting alongside her troops, by the southern wall.

The barrage of falling Titans had eased a short while earlier, but occasionally a new Titan came crashing down.

There was no end in sight, only growing exhaustion. The one saving grace was that none of the Titans were ten-meter-class or larger.

When they fell they wrecked rooftops and smashed through the floors, in most cases bringing the walls and supports with them. Each time great clouds of dust billowed into the air. The Titans' mangled bodies pumped out vapor as they regenerated.

Some residents had been cooking, and fires had broken out in a few neighborhoods. Columns of black smoke rose from these, too. The cannons bombarding the Titans from above also threw up continuous streams of debris.

It was as though Quinta had been swallowed by a many-hued nimbus.

Visibility was poor, and it was almost impossible to keep her eyes open. They grew moist, and overflowed with tears.

Standing at ground level with a blade in each hand, Rita gritted her teeth and gazed up at the wall. The scene was reminiscent of half a year earlier. Then, too, they had resorted to cannon fire to keep the Titans at bay, destroying house after house and scarring the earth with innumerable craters.

But those buildings had been part of an illegal shantytown. These were different. These buildings were sanctioned, inside the wall, yet under relentless fire. They were being blasted apart.

The day had come. The day they were overrun by the Titans.

Most of the residents had already been evacuated to the east wall. The only things left moving were the monsters and the Garrison soldiers.

Yet another five-meter-class was charging in towards her. It had broad shoulders and greasy hair that fell to its shoulders. Its eyes narrowed in a joyful expression, the Titan leaned in over her and stretched its arms.

Rita adjusted the angle on her Vertical Maneuvering Equipment and fired an anchor upwards. It drove into the eaves of the building behind her. Manipulating the trigger, she set the wire to reel in, weaving a path between the Titan's arms and rising to the third floor in no time. The Titan raced on beneath her and crashed into the building with an incredible boom. Still hanging by the wire, Rita was thrown against the wall. She hit it, rebounded, and hit it again. She grimaced, fighting to endure the pain.

"Commander?!" one of the soldiers called out to her, looking up from nearby.

"I'm fine!"

She began to lose height, and unpleasantly hot vapors enveloped her.

The Titan's arm was twisted out of shape and steaming as it lay embedded in the wall, having knocked away part of the building near the corner. The supporting pillar had snapped, and the whole edifice was listing to the side.

The Titan pulled its injured—and rapidly regenerating—arm out from the wall and tilted its head upwards. With the same joyful look, it opened its huge mouth directly below her.

She felt a chill roll down her spine, and her hair stood on end.

"Or maybe not…"

The whole building was tipping now. Rita would be eaten alive if she didn't do something.

She jerked her wrist and pulled the anchor from the building's eaves. She purposely fell feet-first towards the Titan's face.

She threw her legs apart at the last moment, landing with one foot on each of its lips. The Titan's tongue lashed and wriggled below her thighs.

It tried to snap its mouth shut. Rita jumped, somersaulting and brandishing her blades. As she descended toward the creature's back, she cut a hunk of flesh from its neck. A fresh blanket of steam flared out. The Titan went limp, fell to its knees, and tipped headfirst into the half-destroyed building. It plunged right through, seeming to merge with the structure.

Rita landed on the ground and shot an anchor before the rush of debris could hit her. The wire carried her all the way to another building.

Another Titan toppled from the wall, just one block away. The roof of a four-story building was blown to smithereens. Yet more debris and steam spewed out.

The soldier who'd expressed concern for Rita started to dash, no doubt to try and take down the newcomer, but he wasn't wearing the equipment. Lacking the skills, he hadn't been allocated a set.

"I'll take this one, so help anyone still stuck here!"

"O-Okay!"

"Go, now!"

Rita lowered her center of gravity, then fired an anchor in the vicinity of the nearest rooftop. As soon as she felt the impact of the anchor burrowing in, she switched the wire to rewind; as though shoved from behind, she floated into the air.

The building's wall came hurtling in. She pulled the anchor free and kicked off the wall, jumping almost vertically upwards in the direction of the roof. The world opened up, and Quinta spread below her in every direction.

She fired an anchor again, this time at the building next to where the Titan had fallen. Setting the wire to reel in the moment the anchor broke a tile, she pulled herself towards the building, skillfully killing her momentum as she came in to land.

She scrutinized the building ahead of her.

A plume of dust and steam wafted out of a gaping hole in the middle of the flat roof. The Titan in there was relatively small, probably a three-meter-class. At that size, it had plunged through the roof perhaps but not the fourth floor. The moment Rita considered this, a dark shape rose up from inside the steam. The outline began to reshape itself and formed a Titan's head. It was definitely a three-meter-class, standing with only its head protruding through the ceiling.

She wasn't in its visual field as of yet.

Running without any conscious thought, she closed the distance between her and the back of the creature's head.

When she was less than three meters away, the Titan turned to look straight at her. It had tangled black hair and looked awfully sleepy.

Rita stopped herself from hurling a curse and fired an anchor instead. Its end stabbed the Titan between its eyebrows. Its head flinched, moving back a notch.

Without a moment's hesitation, Rita manipulated the trigger. The wire tugged at the Titan's head, forcing its throat into the edge of the hole in the roof. Rita, herself, was drawn up into the air and towards the Titan.

It opened its mouth.

She could see the glossy sheen of its teeth.

A split second before they collided, Rita pulled the anchor free. She kicked off the tiles and sailed over the Titan's head. Before she cleared it, she released the blade in her right hand and took hold of the creature's tangled hair, dampening her inertia. She let go and landed with both feet on the roof, spun a half-circle, and executed two swipes of the blade in her left hand. The strike severed the monster's nape.

The Titan's body turned slack, and its head vanished into the depths of the hole. Moments later steam cascaded out of the opening like a geyser and formed a column.

"Nice."

She'd taken it down with the bare minimum of effort. It was good luck, and didn't happen often.

She crouched and retrieved the blade she'd let go of.

A soldier landed next to her—a young girl, still bearing traces of innocence but already skilled with the Vertical Maneuvering Equipment. The mere fact that she was alive richly testified to her prowess.

"R-Reporting in!" The young girl straightened her posture even as her eyes were drawn to the diminishing column of steam. "All the civilians are now gathered by the east gate. We have all the wagons we could find, positioned at the front."

"How many did you secure?"

"Just over thirty."

It wasn't many, but more than she'd initially hoped. She had to be content.

"We prioritized getting the children into the wagons," the subordinate continued her report.

Rita had given them orders to that effect, but even so… "I'm surprised the adults complied."

"Ah, um…" the soldier stammered for some reason. Maybe they'd had to take forceful measures to bring people into line. Maybe they'd killed someone as an example, and she was balking at delivering the report herself. Whatever the case, Rita would find out when she got there.

"What about Gabriele?" she asked. She'd thought of a use for him after the fight with the Titans had started and issued orders to a nearby subordinate.

The girl soldier nodded enthusiastically. "We managed to track him down. He's in our custody now."

"Next to the gate, I hope?"

"Yes."

"Good work."

Soldiers were still engaged in combat close to Rita. Yet, the Titans' descent appeared to have broken off, at least for now. She could afford to leave the fray without doing much harm with her absence.

"We'll go there together."

Rita broke into a run across the roof. Without hesitation she leapt from the edge and into the air, controlling the Vertical Maneuvering Equipment as she did. She fired her anchors at buildings on either side and swung like a pendulum, yanking her anchors free when her height crested and firing them at the next buildings ahead. This she repeated, carrying herself rapidly through the empty streets.

More and more people appeared below her. They eventually turned into a crowd.

A large number of residents were packed together around the district's gate. Their voices overlapped to give the impression that the earth itself was growling.

In line with her instructions, wagons had been set up in a line before the gate. Some had tarpaulin covers while others didn't. Small children were packed tightly into the latter.

She stood on a rooftop across the road from the gate. A few of the soldiers noticed and acknowledged her presence with their eyes, whether they were on top of the wall or down on the ground. The troops were busy commanding the civilians to queue up calmly.

She realized something. Many of those helping guide the civilians weren't wearing Garrison uniforms. A number were people she recognized, from the teachers association, the butchers union. People who'd been arrested and subsequently released in response to Mathias' appeal—members of the resistance. Scholars, booksellers, many more, were all working hard, hollering at the civilians, urging them to cooperate.

Without the rebels' help, she doubted they could have assigned the wagons to just the children.

It was ironic.

Rita had claimed that people could live in Quinta forever. She had seen the resistance as subversives who undermined law and order. Yet, now that the Titans were here, it was due to their efforts that order was being maintained.

Maybe that was why the girl soldier had hesitated to report the reason.

It meant Rita had been wrong—and Mathias, right.

No, that wasn't true, either.

Mathias' plan had been to appeal to Fuerth for assistance. But Fuerth District lacked any such intention.

Both of their expectations had been proven wrong, and the world was crueler than either of them had supposed.

Rita felt dizzy. She came dangerously close to falling from the roof. She took a hurried step backwards.

She couldn't die yet.

It wasn't as though her principles had been proven wrong.

A lanky young man was arguing with one of her soldiers, ahead of the line of wagons, just in front of the gate. The man's hands were bound behind his back.

Gabriele.

Rita stepped back a little, took a running approach, and leapt into the air. She fired an anchor into the wall that protected the district, set the wire to reel in, and cut straight over the crowd beneath her. As she came back down she kicked both feet off the gate, killing her momentum and coming to rest next to Gabriele.

Caught unawares, he flinched a little. The civilians nearby were watching with wide eyes.

Gabriele threw her a defensive look. "What? What the hell are you planning for me?"

"Oh, nothing too taxing," Rita said in response. "Just for you to steer one of the wagons. The one at the front."

"That's..." He looked over to the wagons, then, realizing Rita's scheme, turned pale. "That's impossible. I told you, you can't come to Fuerth."

"We can't stay here. I think the same applies to you. I'm offering you the use of a wagon."

"As a bargaining chip? You'd give me a wagon, if I took *them*." The children inside the wagons were huddled together, visibly anxious. Some looked sulky, others were openly bawling.

"Yes. That sounds about right."

Gabriele was a Fuerth official and the son of one of the district's luminaries. It was unlikely they would ignore him or turn him away, even if he arrived with a trail of refugees.

"They won't open the gate, you know?"

"Who can say? We've got refugees living there already, lots of them. Who knows what might happen if they find out their own are being kept out?"

They would probably riot. And that would be high on the list of eventualities the royal government wanted to avoid.

"Damn it."

"If you arrive ahead of us, request them to send out their elite. To protect the refugees following behind."

"They'll never do that, all right?!" Gabriele ploughed his hands through his hair. "And, yeah, haven't you considered that I might double-cross you? Who's to say I won't steal one of the horses and race off to Fuerth by myself?"

"I'll be assigning troops to keep watch so that doesn't happen. And to make sure the refugees are safe. Except..." *I'd rather trust you on this.*

Gabriele was a man who put Fuerth's interests first—he hadn't shown the slightest reluctance to poison Bernhardt—but Rita didn't think he was low enough to abandon a few hundred children stowed in wagons.

"Damn... Damn. Damn!" he swore, then started to make his way to the lead wagon. He'd decided to comply, if only to save himself.

Rita nodded at one of her soldiers. He ran after Gabriele, made him stop, and cut the ropes from his arms with a sword.

That would do, for now.

Rita shot an anchor low on the wall, set the wire to reel in, and hauled herself onto the tarpaulin covering one of the wagons. She used the vantage point to study the crowd.

No praising looks—the people watched her without a word, their eyes filled with anger, hate, resentment, contempt.

It was only to be expected.

She'd been draconian. It had all been to keep them safe. Yet her hopes had vanished into thin air as rapidly as a mirage, leaving behind nothing but despair.

She was overtaken with an urge to say something, but decided against it. She feared she'd start mouthing excuses.

Looking away from her people, she caught the eyes of the

soldiers flanking the gate.

"Raise the gate!"

The soldier in charge was flummoxed for a moment, but soon pulled himself together. He turned on his heels and ran into a structure attached to the wall. There came the sound of metal grinding as the chains began to turn; the iron slats that were the gate slowly lifted up.

Light filtered into the dark passageway.

Gabriele whipped his horse before the gate was all the way up. As though waking from a hypnotic state, people began to swarm towards the corridor. None of them paid Rita any more attention. They were all scrambling to get out.

Firing her anchor again, Rita returned to the roof where she'd stood earlier.

The swarm of people moved below her like a turbid stream.

When she looked up, a ghost town lay before her. In the distance, more Titans were diving off the wall. Clouds of debris and steam seethed upwards. Bloody battles were resuming within them.

Rita knew she had to go back, and as soon as possible.

Everything was lost.

The screams, the shouts, the cries of the fleeing civilians somehow seemed so faraway.

The Harsh Mistress of the City

EPILOGUE

It felt as though a hundred—even a thousand—Titans had entered Quinta, but the actual total was less than thirty.

The Garrison troops kept up their fight.

As the battle raged, the vast majority of Quinta's civilians made it through the gate. Those who insisted on staying were left alone.

Come sunset, the whole district was bathed in an eerie quiet.

Many of the soldiers died, but civilian casualties had been kept to a minimum. Most of them escaped Quinta on foot, walking in caravan with the others.

After seeing the last man through, the soldiers closed the gate to imprison the Titans they hadn't been able to take down. They then used their Vertical Maneuvering Equipment to clear the wall and to join the civilians on their desperate flight.

Mathias was bringing up the rear. So were Derek and Jodi. They had—along with a large proportion of the resistance—stayed within the wall until the last possible moment to guide the evacuation. Not even out of a spirit of self-sacrifice, but rather a kind of stubbornness.

Klaus and Nikki were different. When they last spoke with Mathias, the pair were ensconced in the middle of the procession. No doubt they had calculated that leaving too early would put them in danger of being snapped up by Titans in the exterior, while leaving too late would leave them exposed to the Titans already inside the town.

The two outlaws were selfish and rational to the end.

Mathias had told them of Jarratt's predicament, and of Bernhardt's fate. Klaus had merely muttered a cold acknowledgment, as was his wont. Nikki had declared it a shame in her usual carefree manner but had avoided eye contact, gazing into the distance the whole time.

Doris was at the front of the group, it appeared. Mathias heard that she was managing to walk by herself, with only the occasional bit of assistance from the young and fit.

They walked until it was almost dawn, finally ending their march when they were deep within a forest.

The soldiers who had left Quinta first began using their Vertical Maneuvering Equipment to haul the horses and supplies, together with the people themselves, up to the great branches of the tall trees. The plan was to wait off the ground until nightfall, then to move again. Should an aberrant Titan capable of scaling trees or a Colossus taller than the canopy appear, the soldiers would no doubt put their lives on the line.

Mathias squinted into the half-dark, craning to look up once again. Dozens of wires were being wound slowly upwards from spots some tens of meters aboveground. Horses were bound in tight layers of rope. The whole scene looked like some kind of construction site. Scared by the height, some of the children let out muffled cries.

"You need to get us up there!"

"It'll be dawn if you don't get a move on."

Civilians from the tail end of the procession were muttering and complaining all around Mathias, but no one was attempting to cut in. They knew from experience that Rita, or one of the soldiers, would ruthlessly put them to the sword if they did.

Acting spontaneously, they started to sit themselves down.

Mathias was exhausted, but he made a survey of their surroundings anyway. They'd been lucky—no one had sustained severe injuries. Food and water was being passed around. He couldn't see Rita, but he was sure she was there somewhere leading the others in their efforts to lift the civilians and supplies.

He sighed, then found a place apart from the crowd to put his feet up. He was happy to be the last man aloft.

He leaned against a tree, hugged his knees to his chest, and stuck his head between them.

His thoughts kept returning to Rita.

What she was planning to do, if they did make it to Fuerth...

He'd only meant to rest, but fell asleep.

He woke to someone shaking him by the shoulder. The fallen

leaves were now stained by the pale light of dawn. A pair of feet crunched the leaves.

A Titan could show up at any moment.

He felt calm, though.

When he looked up and saw who was standing there, he did feel a little taken aback.

"Rita…"

"Come with me. We've got to get you up there."

At first he couldn't move.

Rita tipped her head to one side. "What's wrong?"

"I don't know. It's just that…" Mathias pressed his hands into the tree behind him, using the support to get to his feet. His joints were stiff and aching slightly. "I guess I'm surprised."

"At what?"

"Your coming in person."

"Why?"

The exhaustion was clear on her features. There was sorrow there too.

Mathias thought for a moment before he answered, "You were going to execute me."

"That was—necessary, at the time. To maintain order. But the town's gone now."

"You don't hold it against me?" He'd killed one of her soldiers. It was only natural if she did.

She responded with a question. "That was an accident, no?"

"It was."

"There's a part of me that can't forgive you for it. But you're helping with the evacuation."

Does she mean she'll treat me as a regular civilian as long as I'm useful and not mete out private justice at this stage?

"That way. It's safer if we're all close together."

Mathias followed her lead. "What do you plan to do after this?" he lobbed the question at her back without even thinking.

She answered still facing forwards. "I'll accept the judgment of the royal government."

"Right, me too."

Mathias had joined forces with criminals in his escape from Fuerth, and people had lost their lives in the process. He would accept whatever punishment he had coming.

"But after that. If…"

"If it isn't the death penalty?" the words flowed easily from Rita's mouth where they had stalled for Mathias.

"Right."

"I'm with the Garrison Regiment. I'll protect the people as long as I'm allowed to."

Her determination always amazed him. Her eyes were already set on the future.

How do I compare to that?

Mathias searched for something he thought he could do, however small, to make himself of use to others.

"I…I think I'd like to represent the refugees. If possible, I'd like to negotiate our position. Communicate our circumstances, our needs, to the central authorities."

Rita said nothing.

Around them, the lifting process was entering its last stages. Mathias could count on his fingers the number of civilians still in view.

Rita came to a stop and looked up. She narrowed her eyes. She set the angle of the firing mechanism and released the anchors of the Vertical Maneuvering Equipment. The sound of metal biting into wood followed. She looked around and extended a hand towards Mathias.

"Take hold, we'll go straight up."

"Okay."

He felt suddenly uneasy.

Was this their last conversation? Was she carrying him to safety now, only to have another soldier bring him down at night?

If they were lucky enough to reach Fuerth, and after accepting their sentences and paying for their crimes, were they going to be strangers for the rest of their lives?

The thought was unbearable.

It didn't matter if it was just once every few days, even once every few weeks, and even if they never laughed together again—he still wanted to see her, to be able to talk to her.

He had no right to wish for such a thing.

He realized that.

And yet, he couldn't stop himself from asking.

"Rita…"

"Hm?"

"Once all this is settled, I want to see you again."

She looked troubled.

Mathias went on. "I'm an idiot, a fool. And I know what I'm about to say is just an excuse. But I think I can do better…if you're around. I can put myself to work for others."

"Why?" Now Rita looked baffled. She also looked as though she might cry. "…When all I've done is mess up?"

"I'll stop you next time," Mathias said. "I swear. I'll be the one to stop you. In return, when I'm about to mess up—"

"Okay."

Rita leaned in a bit and held her arm out further. She hesitated, but finally took hold of his hand.

"I'll stop you, Mathias."

He nodded without saying anything, squeezing her hand in return.

Here are two losers, the thought came to Mathias. *Huddling close, licking each other's wounds. Setting out on their journeys of atonement.*

THE END

The Harsh Mistress of the City

COMMENTARY

For many readers, I think this is our first meeting.

My name is Ukyo Kodachi. I contribute military-related ideas for the main *Attack on Titan* series.

One tie has led to another, and I've been entrusted with the estimable task of commenting on this volume. If you would kindly indulge me, I would be most happy.

The tale called *Attack on Titan* has many essences, but I believe one of them is the idea of resisting.

Today, in the so-called postmodern era, we are all equally exposed to the raging waves of the times.

Ours differ from the Cold War era of the twentieth century. Everyone understood it as an era of nuclear war but turned a blind eye in order to enjoy a modicum of peace.

The kind of ruin that we face now isn't "the certain destruction of nukes" but rather uncertainties that strangle us slowly, be they economic, environmental, or terrorist.

Confronted with ruin, are we not exposed to the heavy pressure of having to choose between "resisting it" and "getting slaughtered"?

Naturally, no matter the region or place, having to resist the times is a universal. The fact that it's not just contemporary but universal—isn't that why *Attack on Titan* became so widely loved?

This novel is, without a doubt, a tale of "resistance": people resisting and confronting a desperate, hopelessly cruel fate.

It's not just that there are giants who devour humans.

On a more basic level, it's about Mathias, Rita, everyone, confronting reality.

They don't fight just because there are Titans, but to fend off calamity itself, on behalf of those trampled underfoot and for their own sakes, losing something by it but gaining something else.

Surely, this more than anything else is proof that we have an *Attack on Titan* piece here.

It concerns what the character called Rita would but could not protect, and what she selects and chooses then. It also concerns what it is that Mathias recovers and gains in the process.

***

I've gone on too long about what captured my feelings.

Now, a little commentary from the angle of military affairs.

A big theme of this book is "defense."

Fighting in defense does wonders for morale. That's because among all wars it's the easiest kind to justify.

You can tell from the fact that "defense" is the justification for most wars. Protecting the people from lawless invaders who threaten the homeland is not a difficult logic to comprehend.

But in reality, defensive fighting is very grueling.

That's because the fighting never "ends."

Not so for the attacking side—if the castle falls, or the other country is made no more, or all the humans in the city are eaten, it ends there.

The defending side has to fight endlessly "until the attackers decide to quit," so there's no breakoff point. Moreover, being on the defensive doesn't guarantee allies or reinforcements. Being unable to acquire anything from the enemy (if you could do that, you'd beat them back), there's the fear that the situation might only deteriorate.

This is evident from modern-day counterterrorism.

Terrorists are able to attack our cities and settlements freely and in their own time. They're elusive, and the attack's cost is far cheaper than the defending side's costs.

But not putting up a guard is not an option. That signifies defeat.

Defensive warfare is always a question of how to keep up that guard and how to suffer a conflict that never ends.

Thus, for both the rank-and-file and their commanders, and

for the civilians too, how to "resist" and how to bring things to a close are tough issues.

The side that repels the enemy and "wins" a defensive war frequently perpetrates gruesome tragedies against itself, shedding blood as freely inside as it did outside.

The reader who traced the path this tale took knows this.

It is not a fight where some overwhelming divine power scorches all of the marauding enemies and nothing is lost.

Something is lost in every battle, order is destroyed, and in the end, the land to be protected might be forfeit itself.

What Mathias and the others decide in the end is one form of this. You could argue they did "defend" what was worth defending or just as well as that they didn't.

Regarding Mathias, you could even say he's only begun to protect.

***

Forgive me that lengthy digression.

The curtain falls on the tale for now, but I hope we meet again.

Please continue to bestow your favor on *Attack on Titan*.

2015, Lucky Day in Spring
Ukyo Kodachi

Author **Ryo Kawakami** is an award-winning novelist as well as a game designer of repute and a member of the Group SNE collective.

Much sought-after illustrator **Range Murata** is also a conceptual designer for animated works and video games and a figure artist.